Finding the Road Home

DIANE GREENWOOD MUIR

This is a work of fiction. Names, characters, places, brands, media, and incidents are either the product of the author's imagination or are used fictitiously. The author acknowledges the trademarked status and trademark owners of various products referenced in this work of fiction, which have been used without permission. The publication / use of these trademarks is not authorized, associated with, or sponsored by the trademark owners.

All rights reserved. No part of this book may be reproduced in any form or by any electronic or mechanical means, including information storage and retrieval systems, without permission in writing from the publisher, except by a reviewer, who may quote brief passages in a review.

Cover Design Photography: Maxim M. Muir

Copyright © 2017 Diane Greenwood Muir
All rights reserved.

ISBN: 1548221996
ISBN-13: 978-1548221997

Don't miss any books in Diane Greenwood Muir's

Bellingwood Series

Diane publishes a new book in this series on the 25th of March, June, September, and December. Short stories are published in between those dates and vignettes are written and published each month in the newsletter.

You can also find a list of all published works at nammynools.com

Journals
(Paperback only)
Find Joy – A Gratitude Journal
Books are Life – A Reading Journal
Capture Your Memories – A Journal

Re-told Bible Stories
(Kindle only)
Abiding Love - the story of Ruth
Abiding Grace - the story of the Prodigal Son

TABLE OF CONTENTS

CONTENTS v
CHAPTER ONE 1
CHAPTER TWO 9
CHAPTER THREE 17
CHAPTER FOUR 25
CHAPTER FIVE 32
CHAPTER SIX 40
CHAPTER SEVEN 48
CHAPTER EIGHT 56
CHAPTER NINE 65
CHAPTER TEN 73
CHAPTER ELEVEN 82
CHAPTER TWELVE 90
CHAPTER THIRTEEN 98
CHAPTER FOURTEEN 107
CHAPTER FIFTEEN 115
THANK YOU FOR READING! 124

CHAPTER ONE

Mid-January

He leaned over and kissed Polly. "Thank you for picking me up."

She patted his knee before putting the car into gear. "No problem. You must be glad to finally be free."

"You have no idea." Joey put his seat belt on. "That was the longest thirty days of my life, but I'm feeling good now. I can't wait to get back to our life. Do you want to go out to dinner tonight? We should celebrate."

"Are you sure?" she asked. "Don't you want to just go home and relax in your own place?"

"I want to be with you." He nodded. "If you really don't mind, I would like to take a long hot shower." He paused and turned to look at her. "By myself. I haven't put up with that much public nudity since I was in grammar school. It was horrid."

"I can't imagine."

"I hope you never have to. If I never see the inside of another jail cell, it will be too soon. Would you mind staying? I'll put on some fresh clothes and we can go out." Joey played a quick rhythm on the dash with his hands. "I feel like eating good food and drinking good wine." With his left hand, he brushed a stray hair back from her temple. "With the most beautiful girl I know."

Polly nodded. "That would be nice. I can't stay out too late though. Tomorrow's my early day."

"I wish you'd quit that job," Joey said. "I can support you. You'd never have to work again."

"Stop it," she said. "We've talked about this too many times. I love my job."

"I know, I know," he responded. "The smell of the books, the interesting people, watching children find joy in reading. Yada. Yada. At least you aren't a dull librarian. You're the most exciting woman I've ever met."

"You need to get out more." Polly made a turn and tapped her brake to avoid hitting a car that darted in front of her.

"Idiot," he said. "You should get up on his ass."

"I'm not doing that. You know what traffic's like."

"Kill or be killed."

She nodded. Boston traffic was different than anything she experienced growing up in Iowa. Not even Des Moines held a candle to this insanity. No matter the time of day or night, the streets were filled with cars. And those damned roundabouts; she still had trouble negotiating them. The first time her father was in the car when Polly got stuck in the middle of one of those things, he'd been pasty white by the time she finally got to the outside and the street she was looking for. He never said a word, though.

"What are you going to do tomorrow?" she asked.

"I have to set up meetings with my parole officer and another anger management counselor. Then I thought I'd run over to the house and see Mother and Father. I'd like them to know that I'm home."

Polly didn't respond to that. Though the Delancys paid for Joey's lawyer, neither of his parents came to the trial and he'd not said anything about them visiting while he was in jail. It was almost as if they refused to believe this had happened. If they closed their eyes to it, the problem might go away. Polly wasn't sure how his mother explained to her society friends that her son had spent thirty days in jail. The truth was, there were plenty of black sheep in every one of those families. Somehow, Joey had managed to get on the wrong side of a judge and his family's money couldn't buy him out of the sentence.

His altercation with the young man at the club had been public, since so many people had recorded it on their cell phones. The worst thing for Joey was that the young man he assaulted was also well-connected in Boston society. It all happened because Polly tripped and the poor kid had the audacity to catch her before she hit the floor. The rest of the evening had been surreal. She'd never experienced anything quite like it.

Joey didn't drink much on a regular basis, but that night he had been celebrating. She couldn't even remember why. When he saw the young man catch her and then speak into her ear so she could hear him over the loud music, Joey flew into a rage. He surprised the young man by grabbing him away from Polly. Before she knew what was happening, he had the man on the floor and was beating the hell out of him, screaming something about assaulting his girlfriend. Two burly security guys finally broke through the crowd and pulled Joey off, but not before he'd broken the kid's nose and eye socket. Joey managed to land a couple of punches on one of the security guards as he flailed about until they subdued him. The police showed up and took Joey to jail. Polly bailed him out because he refused to call his parents.

Polly flinched when Joey touched her cheek.

"Sorry," he said. "I'd never hurt you. Surely you know that. What were you thinking about?"

"Nothing. I'm just glad you're out of there. Maybe things can get back to normal now. I've missed you." As soon as the words were out of her mouth, Polly wondered if she meant them. Her world had been peaceful this last month with him out of the picture. She hadn't looked over her shoulder every time a man spoke to her and she'd enjoyed having more time to herself.

Maybe she just needed to put her foot down and break up with him. She turned another corner and pulled into his driveway.

When she looked at him, he gave her that quirky smile and winked. "I've missed you too. Things are going to be better. I promise. I learned so much while I was away. Now it's time to put it to use."

Her body relaxed. This was the Joey she loved. They had fun together. Some of her favorite moments were the Sunday afternoons they played tourist, chasing down historical sites that she hadn't yet explored. He was surprised at the number of places he'd never visited. After living in the Boston area all his life, he'd never managed to find his way to any of the literary sites until they went together.

They'd toured The Old Manse in Concord, Nathaniel Hawthorne's home for three years. The history of the house was incredible. Built by Ralph Waldo Emerson's grandfather, Hawthorne and his wife moved in as newlyweds. Henry David Thoreau had planted a vegetable garden there for the new couple. Polly was overwhelmed with emotion the first time they took the tour and Joey made sure they returned several times so she could explore it to her satisfaction.

"You're doing it again," he said.

"I'm sorry. I was just thinking about the first time we went out to Concord to the Old Manse."

He grinned. "You were so beautiful. Your eyes glittered with tears as you walked in the front door and my heart swelled with love." Joey stepped out of her car, closed the door and came around to open hers.

He made it very clear the first time they went out together that she would wait for him to open her door. For someone as independent as Polly, that had taken some getting used to, but she learned to appreciate his gallant behavior.

Joey put his hand out and she took it as she turned to put her feet on the ground. "I asked Mother to see that the place was aired out, cleaned, and ready for my arrival today. I hope she remembered."

"I'm sure she did," Polly said. "She's quite efficient."

He held her hand as they walked up the steps. When they reached the front door, Joey took the keys from his pocket and opened it. He pointed to the living room. "I'll just run upstairs and take a quick shower. I shouldn't be any longer than a half hour. If you're hungry, I suspect they've filled the refrigerator as well. Help yourself."

"I'm fine, Joey. Go ahead."

They didn't spend much time at his place. He preferred spending evenings in hers. Joey told her that ensured she would never have to travel through the city alone.

Polly wandered into the living room and found herself in front of his bookshelves. She couldn't help herself. Books were like a magnet and a room with bookshelves filled to overflowing was impossible to resist. She'd looked through Joey's books before, but there was never enough time for her to really dig in and see what he had.

Since Nathaniel Hawthorne had been on her mind, Polly scanned the shelves. Joey's books were perfectly organized and she found Hawthorne's *Scarlet Letter*. She put her hand up to draw it off the shelf and stopped herself. He had an old, cloth-bound copy of the book sitting beside a newer copy. Holding her breath, she took the old book into her hands and opened the cover, gasping when she realized that she was holding a first edition. How had he gotten something like this and why had he never told her? This had to be worth ten or twenty thousand dollars.

Polly's hands trembled as she gently turned a few pages. The library had expensive first editions of books on display, but she'd never thought to hold anything like this. Putting it back on the shelf where she'd found it, Polly stepped back. Leaning on the wing of a chair, she looked more closely at the books in front of her. Beside another paperback was an old copy of Charles Dickens's *Oliver Twist*. Polly took it down and shook her head. Another first edition. How many of these things were on the shelves?

Joey knew how much she loved to read and how important

books were to her. Why would he withhold these treasures? It made absolutely no sense.

She opened the book and smiled at the author's name. "Boz" - Dickens's nickname. This was fantastic.

"I didn't expect you to find that so quickly," Joey said.

He was close enough that she could feel his breath against her hair. She hadn't heard him come into the room.

Polly took a step away and turned, holding the book out to him. "I'm sorry. I was snooping. I couldn't help myself."

"How many did you find?"

"Just this and Hawthorne's *Scarlet Letter*. I didn't know you collected first editions."

"Someday these could be yours, you know. I started purchasing them after I met you. I told Mother they would make a wonderful wedding gift."

She continued to hold the book out, so he took it and returned it to its place.

"No comment?"

"I don't know what to say. Those are beautiful books to own. Congratulations on finding them."

"It's not that difficult if you have the money. Now what say we take a drive over to Concord to that fish market you love so much."

"Oh let's not," Polly said. "Not today."

He bounced on his feet. "I want to do something. I'm completely energized. I don't have to smell anyone else's stink around me. I don't have to listen to idiots snoring and grunting all night long. I don't have anyone watching my every move. Let's do something fun." He headed for the front door. "I know. Let's do something touristy. Something we haven't done in a while."

"Joey, I can't be out late. I already told you that I need to be at work early tomorrow morning. Why don't we just eat at a nice restaurant, then I'll bring you back here and go home."

"You know I don't like it when you drive these streets after dark. It's not safe for you to be out alone. Tell you what. How about I follow you home and we'll order a pizza. We can have a quiet evening in and this weekend we'll travel. Maybe we could drive down to the Cape. We haven't visited the lighthouses yet. You'd like that."

Polly and Sal had gone to Cape Cod several times when they were in college. They'd seen several lighthouses at Polly's insistence, but now didn't seem to be the right time to challenge him.

She smiled up at him. "That sounds terrific. Are you sure you want to make the trip all the way over to my place?"

"Honey, I'm free. I would follow you all the way to Iowa tonight if that's where you were going. Go on ahead while there's still plenty of light out. I want to make a couple of stops. Order pizza when you get home and I'll be there soon enough. You know what I like."

Polly nodded and headed for the front door. Joey took her arm and turned her to kiss her lips.

"Those taste wonderful," he said. "Like heaven on earth. I've missed you so much."

"I've missed you too." Polly took his hand and squeezed it, then slipped out the front door. She hoped that it wasn't a mistake inviting him to her apartment tonight. She didn't usually have trouble getting him to leave at a decent hour, but after a month in jail, he was probably ready to spend time with nearly anybody but his cell mates. She backed out of his driveway as the garage door opened.

Joey waved and she returned it, then drove off toward home.

Her phone buzzed and she grinned at seeing Sal's picture pop up. A quick press of the button and Sal's voice came over the speakers in her car.

"I figured you wouldn't answer the call if you were still with him," Sal said. "Is everything okay?"

"It's terrific," Polly responded. "He's good. He's happy and he's so sweet. He's coming back to my apartment and we're going to have dinner in. I think we're going to Cape Cod this weekend. He wants to show me the lighthouses."

"You didn't tell him that you've already been there with me?"

Polly laughed. "No. If he wants to show me around, I'll let him. He has so much fun describing the history of these things. It's kinda sweet."

"So he didn't come out of prison with tattoos or anything?" Sal let out a cackle.

"I don't think so," Polly said. "If they aren't obvious, I'm not prepared to look for them, that's for sure."

"Why not? You could have fun with that."

Polly flipped her blinker on and slowed to make a turn. She wasn't sure why she wasn't excited about pursuing a more physical relationship with Joey. For a long time she chalked it up to not knowing him well enough, but after bailing him out of jail and being there for him during his thirty day sentence, that was no longer the issue. She knew him quite well now. He'd certainly love taking things deeper, but she wasn't ready at all.

"You drive," Sal said. "I can tell you're not paying attention to me. Will you have time for lunch on Friday?"

"I'd love to."

"Drive safe and be good tonight."

"Stop it. I'll talk to you later."

Polly ended the call and smiled. She didn't know where she'd be without Sal.

CHAPTER TWO

Early February

As she walked into the apartment, Polly's phone buzzed with another call from Joey. After those thirty days in jail, he'd become clingy to the point of driving her crazy. He wanted to do something with her every evening and had even taken to begging her to meet for lunch. She felt smothered and had no idea how to tell him. At least tonight she had a good excuse.

"Hello, Joey," she said.

"Just checking in. How was the rest of your day?"

"It was good."

"No funny stories about your goofy patrons? Come on. Not even one?"

"It was a pretty quiet afternoon. I can't talk right now. You know I'm going over to the Renaldi's house for dinner. Drea is going to be here in less than a half hour and I have to change."

"You'll have to take me with you sometime. I'd love to meet Drea's mother. She sounds like quite a character. I suppose the brothers will be there, too."

"I don't know," Polly said. She sat on the arm of the sofa to take off her shoes. "I didn't ask."

"I think the older one likes you. What's his name? Ray?"

"He's like a brother," Polly said. "Both of them are. Now I really need to go. I'll talk to you tomorrow."

"Why don't you call me when you get home tonight?"

Polly stifled a loud sigh. "No. I'll probably just come right home and go to sleep. You know, another early day tomorrow."

"Then meet me at our cafe for lunch tomorrow. I miss you. Please?"

Anything to get him moving. "Sure. That sounds great. I'll meet you there at eleven thirty. Okay?"

"Perfect. Have fun tonight and don't let those brothers get too close to you."

"Good night, Joey. I'll see you tomorrow."

Before he could start something else, Polly ended the call, turned the phone to silent and put it on the end table. She really did need to hurry.

For an evening at Mama Renaldi's house, you dressed up. It was expected. That meant a skirt and blouse. Not even nice pants would do. Of course, Drea's mother would never say anything directly about it, but she'd make remarks about how casual things had become these days or how tragic it was that girls felt the need to behave like men. Talk about old school.

Polly put on a trim black skirt and slipped her feet into a pair of black pumps. The evening Drea had a rather firm discussion with her mother about stockings had been a little embarrassing. Drea had made sure to let Polly know about wearing a skirt, but it had occurred to neither of them that Mama would make a scene about stockings. The funny thing was, the older woman took Polly aside before she left and assured her that she had beautiful legs and did not need to cover them up with those cheap panty hose. Unless she had access to pure silk stockings, she might as well show off her beautiful legs. Polly hadn't been sure what to do with that conversation, but Drea assured her that she was safe in bare legs now. Mama liked Polly enough to change her own mind.

A sharp rap at Polly's door made her jump and she tugged a sweater over her head before running out to see who was there.

"You might be too warm in that sweater," Drea said. "Remember where you're going."

"Am I late? I'm sorry."

"No. I'm a little early. Go put something else on. Ray says Mama's been turning the heat up higher and higher lately."

"Thank you." Polly dashed into her room and flipped through the blouses in her closet. She landed on a pretty blue print she'd picked up at Filene's when she was shopping with Sal, and grabbed a light-weight blue cardigan. That should take care of any contingency.

"Are your brothers going to be at dinner tonight?" Polly asked Drea as they left the apartment.

"Of course they are. If Polly's coming, both of them will be there. They are in love with you."

Drea's brothers were drop dead gorgeous, but treated Polly like they treated their sister and it drove her nuts. Okay, Ray made sense. He was gay. She could live with that, but Jon? She couldn't figure out why it was so easy for him to date every woman under the sun, but pay no attention to her. She tried not to throw herself at him, but sometimes she couldn't help the outright flirting.

"How are things going with Joey now that he's out of jail?" Drea asked.

"They're okay, I guess," Polly responded.

Drea backed out of the parking space and turned to Polly. "What does that mean?"

"It will get better. He just hasn't gotten over the whole jail experience. It's like he lost all of his self-confidence and always has to be with me."

"Feeling a little claustrophobic?"

"Maybe. Yeah. That's probably it. But once he gets back into the swing of his life, we'll go back to normal. We had a great time down at Cape Cod a couple of weeks ago. He wanted to go to Vermont last weekend, but I had to work."

Drea chuckled. "You don't usually work on the weekends. Did you volunteer?"

"Mimi wanted the weekend off. It was no big deal."

"Whatever you say. So are you going to marry this guy?"

"No!" Polly flinched when she realized how loudly she'd said that. "I mean, no. I have no desire to get married to anyone right now. Where'd that come from?"

"It's just that you took care of him through that whole trial and everything. His parents weren't even there for him. That was kind of a big commitment."

"I'd do that for any of my friends." Polly swatted Drea's arm. "But don't test me. I don't ever want to bail you out of jail."

"Don't even bother. If something happens and I'm tossed into jail, just let me rot there. I wouldn't want to have to face Mama, much less Jon and Ray." She chuckled. "They know enough people on the force that they'd probably have me locked in solitary just to teach me a lesson." Drea put her hand up. "I don't intend to ever find out what would happen. Can you even imagine that?"

"I can't. How scary. I can't imagine how scared Joey had to be. He'd never been in any trouble before. Ever. How do you go from being a normal, everyday guy to sitting in a jail cell? He didn't even want his parents to know." Polly pursed her lips. "Heck, I'm sure they know judges that could have gotten him released."

"People are weird."

"His family *is* pretty odd," Polly said. She relaxed as Drea drove. Her mother lived in South Medford in a cozy little red house with blue and teal trim. She idly watched the scenery go by as she thought about marriage. Some days it felt like life was just passing her by. She didn't really have any ties anywhere right now. After her father died, Polly assumed she would live in Boston for the rest of her life, but so far, she hadn't made a move to put roots down. The inheritance he left was more than enough money to buy a condo or a small house somewhere outside the city. Polly couldn't believe how expensive it was to live out here. And sure, she wanted to get married someday, but certainly not to

Joey. At least she didn't think so. Could she be married to Joey? His mother would make her life miserable. Polly wasn't interested in becoming a charity ball attending socialite. That sounded dreadful. It might work for a lot of women, but not for Polly.

"We're here."

Polly startled awake. "I'm so sorry. I can't believe I fell asleep. How long was I out?"

"Only about fifteen minutes." Drea tugged at Polly's cardigan. "You're going to want to make sure you don't wear this to dinner. If you get too warm, you'll fall asleep and do a face plant in your pasta."

"I'm sure your mother would love that. I'm so sorry."

"It's really no big deal. You were tired. Haven't you been sleeping?"

"Joey comes over and stays late. It takes a lot of work to get him to leave. I start about nine thirty and it's usually after midnight before I finally get him out the front door."

Drea stepped out of her car and leaned back in. "You've gotta figure this out, girlfriend. Come on. Ray's already here."

Walking into the Renaldi home was like being embraced in a warm hug. The smell of garlic and seasonings coming from the kitchen combined with the seventy-five-degree base temperature that Mama Renaldi insisted was her comfort zone made Polly take a deep breath and smile.

"There's my girl," Ray said, coming out of the dining room.

Drea walked right up to him and put her arms out for a hug. When he passed her and headed straight for Polly, she laughed out loud. "You never get tired of that, do you? I'm telling Mama."

He gave Polly a quick hug, then picked his sister up into a bear hug.

With her feet dangling, she squirmed in his arms. "Put me down."

"You complained. I fixed it. Stop complaining."

"Is that my favorite daughter?" Drea's mother came out of the kitchen, the epitome of everything Polly imagined an Italian mother should be. Holding a wooden spoon dripping with red sauce in one hand and a wet cloth to catch the drips in the other, she stopped just short of the living room carpeting, pushed her head forward, and turned her cheek. "Give me a quick kiss, dear, and come help me finish dinner." She turned to Polly. "Sweetheart, you are radiant. It is so good to see you tonight. Ray, take her sweater and make her feel comfortable. The wine has breathed long enough."

"Yes, Mama," he said.

Polly let him help her with the sweater. "I can't believe you let that little woman boss you around like that. You're a wuss."

"Little woman? She's six feet tall and three hundred pounds of muscle as far as I'm concerned."

In reality, Mrs. Renaldi was short and petite. Her hair was still jet black, though Polly had an inkling that there was a stylist in town who helped with that. She was a spit-fire and when she was mad at one of her sons, moved faster than lightning to rap their heads. Polly watched it happen one night. Before Jon could get his hand up to protect himself, she'd given him a quick swat and was already headed back to her seat.

The front door opened again and Polly turned to see the other heart-stoppingly beautiful Renaldi brother walk in.

"Polly!" Jon cried and swooped her off her feet. "I've missed you. When are you going to stop chasing those other men and settle down with me? We'd make beautiful babies."

"Leave her alone," Mama Renaldi called from the kitchen. "She's worth ten of you, Jon Renaldi. Now get out here and give your mother a kiss. Ray, have you given Polly a glass of wine? You might as well take a seat at the table. We'll be ready to eat in a few minutes. Jon! Now!"

He giggled and gave Polly a quick peck on the cheek. "I'd better hurry. We'll talk about babies later."

Ray took Polly's arm and escorted her to the dining room, then held out the chair she traditionally sat in. "How are things at the library?"

"It's good. I love it there." She craned her neck to watch him. "There's always something interesting going on."

"How's your physicist friend?"

"Mr. Meara?"

"The one who won't talk to you?"

"He comes in every few days. He must have my schedule figured out. Poor guy. It's so hard for him to talk to people."

"You said that. But he talks to you?"

Polly tilted her head. "No. He really doesn't talk very much. He usually has a list of books that he wants to read. When I see him, I move to the far end of the counter away from the others so he can give me the list. I've found it's easier for me to walk around the library with him. I keep trying to tell him that if he would just send me an email, I'd make sure the books were ready for him to pick up. He's so uncomfortable being around people. I'll do anything to help him."

"But he's not uncomfortable around you, is he?"

"I guess not." She shrugged. "I like him. He always gives me this small smile when I walk us right up to one of the books he needs."

Ray sat down beside her and put a glass of red wine on the table. "How are things with your boyfriend now that he's out of jail?"

"It's okay." Polly was always nervous talking to Ray about Joey. Neither of Drea's brothers was fond of her boyfriend. They thought he was a creep. She wasn't sure how they knew so much about him, but they knew enough. She wished that her friends could see the Joey that she knew.

"If he ever hurts you …"

Polly put her hand on his knee. "He has never come close to hurting me. He just gets jealous. He's very sweet to me."

"Well, if you ever need me, all you have to do is call. I'll be right there."

"I know," she said, smiling at him. "You're wonderful."

Drea came into the dining room bearing two baskets of bread. Polly could smell the garlic before she made it to the table.

"Insalata," Jon said. He placed the large bowl of salad on the table and went back into the kitchen. "I got the antipasti, Mama."

"She's really doing it up," Polly whispered to Drea.

"It's something about Ray heading out of the country tomorrow."

"Where are you going, Ray?" Polly asked.

"Just over to England for a couple of days. Got a job there, but I'll be back soon. Going to miss me?"

Jon put small plates at each place filled with tomatoes, olives and large chunks of mozzarella, then went back into the kitchen only to re-emerge following his mother. He was carrying an immense covered tureen that he placed in front of Ray. "You get to do the honors tonight, big brother."

"Bow your heads," Mama said. She looked around the table and Polly quickly bowed her head and shut her eyes as the older woman said, "Bless us O Lord, and these thy gifts which we are about to receive from thy bounty, through Christ our Lord, Amen."

"Mama? Your glass?" Ray put his hand out.

"You're a good boy," she said.

"What about me?" Jon asked.

His mother reached over and tweaked his cheek. "You are a good boy, too, my son. Thank you for helping me serve tonight. If you'd been here earlier like your brother was, you could have helped me prepare the meal, but at least you showed up." Her eyes twinkled as she smiled at Polly. "Gotta keep these boys humble. They're too pretty for their own good."

CHAPTER THREE

Polly spent most of the next morning helping people at the library's computer stations. She did not get paid enough to put up with some of the stupid things people asked her to help with, but it was still her job. At eleven fifteen, she took a deep breath and headed back to the staff room to get her jacket. When she checked her phone, there were already five texts from Joey. This was ridiculous. She scanned through them to make sure he wasn't canceling their lunch date. No, he was just telling her how much he missed her and couldn't wait to see her. That boy needed to get back to work full-time. This wore her out.

When Polly walked the aisles, by habit, she scanned the shelves just to make sure books were neat and in place.

"Excuse me, Miss Giller?"

She stopped herself and focused on the man in front of her. "Hello. Can I help you?"

"No, I wanted to tell you thank you for the book you recommended last week - on art and war? You were right. I should have read that a long time ago. The author really stirred some things up inside me. Talk about inspiring."

"I'm glad. I've read it a couple of times." Polly chuckled. "To be honest, I took notes the last time I read it. The author makes you feel like there's nothing you can't do if you just set aside your fears."

"Resistance, you mean." He grinned when he said it. "Gotta break through the resistance and everything is possible."

She nodded. "I'm glad you liked the book. What's your art?"

"I've started two screen plays and last night I finished one of them. It's not perfect, but I'm excited to have it done. It's been sitting there for three years. I'm working on the other right now. This afternoon I'm calling a friend who knows someone who will read through them and help me clean them up." He lifted his shoulders. "I'm really excited. I just wanted to say thank you for your help and for taking time to listen to me."

"Well, when you're a famous Hollywood writer, don't forget me," Polly said. She shook his hand and stepped behind the counter.

"He was cute," Janet said. "What did he want?"

Polly shook her head. "Nothing much. Just to say thanks for a book recommendation. I'm heading out for lunch. Back in an hour."

"With your cute boyfriend? What is his name?"

"Joey." This girl drove Polly absolutely crazy. She was as flighty as they came and didn't pay attention to anything anyone said. Polly figured that the only way she kept her job was she had to be related to someone. The rest of the staff wasn't terribly nice to Janet. She got the worst jobs, but she didn't seem to mind. At least she didn't act as if she minded.

"Hey, Polly," Janet called out as Polly walked away.

"What's up?"

Janet ran up to her and held out a ten-dollar bill. "Would you mind bringing me back a tuna on rye? It's kind of cold and I'd rather not go out if I didn't have to."

Polly took the money. "Sure. Anything else?"

"No. Just the sandwich. Thanks." Janet turned on the balls of her feet and pranced back to the counter.

"They're going to have to wrap it up tightly so I can't spit on it," Polly muttered, heading out into the hallway.

She tucked the ten dollars into a back pocket and braced herself before opening the door to go outside. It was cold and the wind had picked up. Fortunately, she only had a couple of blocks to walk.

"You stay away from her!"

Polly turned at the sound of shouting.

"What are you doing?" she yelled, running toward Joey.

He had someone shoved up against the wall of the building and was standing only inches in front of him, red-faced and screaming. Polly panicked when she realized that it was the young man she'd just spoken with in the library.

"Joey, stop!" She grabbed Joey's arm to pull him away.

"You go near her ever again," Joey shouted, "and I'll hurt you." He yanked the briefcase from the man's hands and flung it to the side. "Do you understand what I'm saying to you? Stay away from her!"

Polly pulled Joey's arm. "What are you doing? Stop it. Leave this man alone."

"I will not leave him alone. He can't be allowed near you."

She took a deep breath and pushed an arm between Joey and the man, then wiggled herself between them enough to get her hands on Joey's chest. Little by little she pushed him back until she got enough space to give him a shove. "Back the hell off, you freakin' idiot."

Joey backed up and shook his head, startled at her behavior. Several bystanders had gathered and one man put his hand on Joey's shoulder.

"Back off, asshole," Joey said, shaking the man's hand away.

Polly bent over and picked up the briefcase, never taking her eyes off Joey. She brushed it off, then pointed at a bench twenty feet or so away from them. "You go sit there and wait for me."

Joey opened his mouth to protest and she put her hand up. "I'm not kidding. Get the hell out of here right now. Go. Sit. I'll be there in a minute."

"I don't want to leave you alone with this man," Joey said.

"He's not the one you should be worried about. Leave now." Polly fairly spat the last words at him. She was so damned angry, she just wanted to run.

He finally walked toward the bench, turning with every step to see what she was doing.

"I'm so sorry," Polly said. She wanted to touch the man's arm ... to make a connection, but didn't dare, knowing what Joey was capable of.

"You know him?" the young man asked.

She handed him the brief case and backed up two steps. "Yeah. I guess. I can't believe this happened to you. I don't know how else to say I'm sorry. Are you okay?"

"Yeah. What's his problem?"

"Did he follow you out of the library?"

The young man nodded. "Yeah. He said hello and even held the front door open for me. We walked a few steps and before I knew what hit me, he had me up against the wall. You got here before I could react. I didn't want to hurt him, but he was about to go down."

"I am so sorry. He must have seen us talking."

"He's that mad because we had a conversation? That's nuts."

"I know," she said, closing her eyes as she shuddered. "Are you sure you're okay?"

"I'm fine. But you need to think about what you're doing - being with someone like that," the young man said. "For now, I'll just use a different branch. This was crazy. Somebody needs to lock him up." He shot one glance toward Joey, then turned and went the other way.

Polly bent her head forward and took a few deep breaths. When she looked up, there were still a few people watching her. "I'm fine," she said. "No worries."

Heading for the bench where Joey sat watching her approach, Polly steeled herself. She was done.

"Come on," she said, not even stopping to look at him. "Let's get lunch."

He walked up beside her, reaching for her hand. Polly shoved it into the pocket of her jacket.

"Polly," he whined. "Come on. Hold my hand."

"Not gonna," she hissed. "Shut up until we're somewhere we can talk."

"Why are you so upset? I was just protecting you."

She kept moving, not wanting to look at him; her anger nearly at the boiling point. "I said shut up. I don't want to hear your voice right now."

"What were you two talking about down there? Did he ask you out on a date?" Joey grabbed at her arm. "Is he going to show back up at the library this afternoon and try to see you again?"

Polly stopped, spun on him and wrapped her hand around his forearm. She released it when he winced. "I was trying to make sure that you hadn't hurt him … that he was okay. You are a goddamned idiot. You just got out of jail for hurting someone who had done nothing wrong and now here you are again, pushing and shoving some poor guy whose name I don't even know. I ask you to shut up and you can't even do that. Damn it, Joey. What in the hell is wrong with you?"

She stalked off. They only had another block to the cafe. At this point, she didn't want to go inside, but she sure as hell wasn't going anywhere more private with this idiot.

Joey caught up to her and reached the cafe in time to hold the front door open for her. By that time, she'd breathed enough to calm down. They were regulars here and the waitress waved them in, knowing they'd find a place to sit. Polly looked around and found a table tucked into a corner.

"Why are you so mad, honey?" Joey held the chair for her.

"Because you were unreasonable out there, one." She held up her index finger. Holding up the second finger, she said, "And two, you were spying on me in the library. Are you kidding me with that? It's my job. It's where I work. Why didn't you let me know you were there?" Polly held up a third finger and Joey took her hand, bringing it back down to the table. When she looked up, the waitress was standing in front of them.

"I just want a diet Dew," Polly said.

"And you, sir?"

He left his hand on Polly's and looked up. "Water for me. Bring us each a roast beef on whole wheat. Lettuce, tomato and mayo. Do you want chips?"

Polly was so shocked that he'd ordered for her she couldn't make sense of what she'd just heard come out of his mouth. "Uh. Yeah. Chips."

"Anything else?"

"That will be fine," Joey said. "Bring the drinks when the sandwich is ready and don't bother us otherwise. We need to talk."

The waitress nodded and Polly yanked her hand away from him. "What was that?"

"It's what you usually order. I wanted her to go away so we could talk. I think we should move in together."

Polly opened her mouth and found that she couldn't form words. She pursed her lips, shut her eyes and took a long breath in and then back out. When that didn't make things better, she repeated it twice more.

"No," she said quietly, pushing back rage that begged to explode. "Not now. Not ever. What in the hell happened out there? I thought you were taking anger management courses."

"I'm not doing that any longer," Joey said. "I don't need those."

"Apparently, you do. What did your counselor say when you told him you were quitting the classes?"

He shrugged. "I'm not seeing him either. He wasn't doing me any good. I've got this. Really. Don't worry about it."

"I don't think you do, Joey," Polly said. "I don't think you do at all. What you did out there today was beyond the pale. You don't just threaten someone because I speak to them. I talk to people all day long - both men and women. You can't threaten them all."

"But *he* was a threat to you."

"No, Joey, he wasn't. He was just a nice guy who stopped to say thank you for a book recommendation. That's all. I don't even know his name." She pushed her chair away from him. "I think we're done."

"What?" Joey looked at her in a panic. "What do you mean we're done?"

"I mean that I'm breaking up with you. I can't take this anymore. You are not good when you're with me."

"That's the only time that I'm any good," he protested. Tears filled his eyes. "You can't leave me. I promise to go back and see the counselor. I'll do whatever you want."

"No you won't," Polly said. "You knew that I wanted you to stay with your counselor and you quit. If you go back, you'll do it only until you think that you're in control again and then you'll stop. You aren't trying to fix this, you're trying to control it."

"Please don't," he whimpered. "Please. I'm nothing without you. You are my light. During those dark days in jail, the only thing that got me through was knowing you were waiting for me. When I saw you the day you picked me up, all the cares that had weighed me down were lifted off my shoulders. Please don't leave me." Joey reached for her hand and took it in his.

Polly realized that his touch made her ill. She yanked her hand back as the waitress approached with a tray.

She set down their drinks and then the two sandwiches and chips. "Anything else?"

Polly shook her head. "That's it. Thanks."

"I'll just leave the ticket, then."

"Thank you." Polly nodded.

Joey had braced his hands on his knees and was looking at the floor. "You can't leave me," he said, pleading. "You just can't. We're perfect together. Please give me another chance. I will do anything. Anything."

Taking a drink of her soda, Polly tried to decide how much of this she wanted to deal with. He disgusted her. He scared her. He was out of control. Drea's family tried to warn her, Sal didn't like him much and now, even a stranger she only knew from the library attempted to warn her away from this nutcase. She needed to end it.

"I'm done, Joey. You can't fix this. We should not be together."

"Please tell me this isn't the end," he said. "You can't let it fall apart just because I screwed up."

"Yes, I can." Polly stood, took out the ten-dollar bill that Janet had given her and tossed it on the table. She'd deal with that later. "Don't ever call me again."

She shoved her chair back in and walked out. Fortunately, a taxi stopped immediately. She jumped in the back seat, gave him her home address, then took out her phone and made a quick call.

"Boston Public Library. Mrs. Gavin's office."

"This is Polly Giller. Could I speak with Mrs. Gavin?"

"Just a moment, please."

"Hello, Polly. What's up?" The older woman wasn't a close friend, but Polly trusted her.

"I'm sorry, Mrs. Gavin. I never do this, but I'm so sick. Can I take the rest of the day off?"

There was a pause. Polly knew she'd confused the woman. She had never taken a sick day.

"Are you okay?"

"Yeah. I'll be in tomorrow. I'm sorry about this."

"I'm worried about you, Polly."

"Please don't worry. I just need to take care of a few things and I'll feel much better. Is this all right?"

"Of course it is, as long as you aren't going to the hospital."

"No. I'm sorry, though."

"Don't worry. Go home and take care of yourself. Let us know if you need anything."

"Thank you. I will."

Polly ended the call and called a locksmith not far from her home. When she explained what she needed, he agreed to meet her there to change out the locks.

Her phone rang. Polly saw Joey's name and rejected the call. He tried again and again until she finally turned the phone off.

As soon as the locks were changed, she was getting a new phone number. She couldn't take this.

CHAPTER FOUR

Polly stood in the shower the next morning, praying that she'd be able to shake off a night with very little sleep. Mrs. Gavin was going to want to know what was wrong and Polly wasn't ready to tell anyone.

All night long, she'd played out hundreds of scenarios in her mind. She worried that the young man Joey assaulted would sue her or the library. She worried that Joey would show up at the library and make a scene. She was terrified that she'd open her front door this morning and find him there, begging her to take him back.

It had taken most of the night, but Polly finally concluded that she had no qualms about calling the police if he harassed her. After his thirty-day stint in jail, a judge wouldn't hesitate to get him out of her way, especially since she was about the only person who might bail him out. Nobody else in Joey's life would expend energy or money on him.

Polly was also certain that if she called Jon or Ray Renaldi, Joey wouldn't have a chance. He'd probably find himself stranded on a desert island in the middle of the Pacific Ocean the next morning.

That thought made her laugh out loud. She wasn't ready to call them, though. They'd made it clear that she shouldn't have been with Joey in the first place. Admitting how badly she screwed this up wasn't at the top of her list of things to do today. Maybe tomorrow. But definitely not today.

After doing a quick cleanup, Polly put her coat on and headed for the front door. As soon as she put her hands in her pocket, she realized that, though she had her keys, she'd left her car at the library yesterday afternoon. She was thankful that taxi driver had pulled up just when she needed an immediate escape, but that didn't help her this morning.

She sat down on the arm of the sofa and took out her phone. It was probably just as well. Not facing insane traffic when she could barely function was a good idea.

After making the call, Polly slid down onto the sofa and turned the television back on. She idly flipped through channels, not paying any attention to what was playing. Throughout the night, the one person Polly hadn't allowed herself to think about was her father. It wasn't that he'd be disappointed in her, but just thinking about how badly she wanted him to help her through this made Polly's eyes fill with tears. She brushed them away.

"No you don't. Not now. You can fall apart later. You have to get through this day." Polly swung her legs around to the front of the sofa, sat up straight, and turned off the television. If she wasn't going to find something to watch, she needed to move on. The taxi would be here soon anyway.

She went into the kitchen and opened the refrigerator. Nothing new would have arrived since her forage at five thirty this morning. She'd finished leftover pizza at that hour, calling it breakfast. She was really looking for something to make for lunch. The cafe that she enjoyed so much was now off-limits. That annoyed her, but there was no way she was going back. Not after she'd stalked out in a snit yesterday.

Huffing a laugh, she looked up. "I know, Mary. Nobody was paying any attention to me. They all have their own lives and I wasn't even a blip in their day."

The woman who cared for Polly after her mother died, Mary Shore, was a practical, straightforward woman. She and her husband, Sylvester, were friends of Everett and Barbara Giller. Sylvester worked with Polly's dad on the farm for as long as Polly could remember. Mary had been a receptionist until Barbara died. Knowing how badly his little girl needed a woman in her life, Everett hired Mary to be in the home while he worked in the fields. She was there every morning when Polly got up and in the afternoons when Polly came home from school. Mary had been exactly what was needed to help Polly through that horrible time. The Shores never had children of their own, so she loved Polly with everything she had.

Polly couldn't begin to imagine what life would have been like without that wonderful woman there to care for her. It had been Mary who called when Polly's dad was killed. They'd talked on the phone for several hours that night as Polly worked through guilt at not living in Iowa so she could be close to her father. Mary's silent permission allowed Polly to express devastation at the loss of her father. In those moments when Polly was ready to toss everything up in the air and move home, it had been Mary's practical love that reminded Polly she was living a life her father wanted for her. There could be no regret; only gratitude for the life they'd had together.

Losing Mary a year and a half later hadn't been easy. With no ties holding her to Iowa, Polly threw herself into her life in Boston. Everett's brother, Clyde, wanted nothing to do with Polly. She'd never understood that and her father wouldn't talk about it. There had been quite a bit of tension between the brothers when Everett retired from farming after Sylvester Shore died of a heart attack. He was too young and Everett decided to make some changes to his own life. He didn't want to hire anyone else and start over, so he sold everything to his brother, moved into a little house in town, and set up a workshop in his garage. He was happy and relaxed; more so than Polly had ever known him to be. Mary had gone over to help him around the house and was always there whenever Polly returned for holidays and vacations.

The sound of a horn honking broke Polly from her reverie. She smiled. There wasn't a time that she didn't enjoy getting lost in memories of her family. It wasn't a normal family, but it had been perfect. She made sure all the lights were off, patted her jacket pocket once again to make sure the keys were there and opened the front door.

"What the hell is this?" she snarled.

A large bouquet of roses had been placed on the threshold of her door. Polly desperately wanted to give it a swift kick, but instead, picked it up and pulled the door shut behind her. Her first thought was to toss the roses in the garbage bin, but she stopped herself. She was too thrifty for that, even if Joey completely disgusted her. Throwing perfectly good things in the trash was never easy for her. Both Mary and Everett had taught her that.

"Good morning," the taxi driver said as Polly got into the car.

"Hello."

"Flowers from your beau?"

Polly looked at the roses she was carrying and took a breath. "Yeah."

"Must have been a big fight. Either that or it's your birthday or anniversary."

When Polly simply nodded, the woman put the car into reverse. "Where are you going this morning?"

Polly gave her the address and sat back, then wondered how long the flowers had been lying in front of her door. They couldn't have been there too long, so she glanced around furtively, wondering if Joey was still there, watching her. She gave a quick shudder and swallowed back bile. He wasn't going to intimidate her. The last thing she wanted to do was waste time worrying about him. She'd told herself over and over throughout the night that she wasn't afraid to call the police. He couldn't hurt her.

Well, to be honest, he *couldn't* hurt her. She chuckled quietly. The guy was such a wimp if someone pushed back. He thought he was a big deal, but if that young man yesterday had wanted to, he could have put Joey on the ground and destroyed him. Polly was fairly certain that if Joey threatened her physically she could also destroy him. The night in the bar had been a fluke. Alcohol had removed his sense of self-protection and he'd lost control.

Joey had gotten playful a couple of times in the past and tried to wrestle with her. The first time, she let him win - you know, being the nice girl and all. The next time, a few weeks later, he tried again when Polly wasn't ready for it and she'd pushed him off and to the ground before stalking into the bathroom to cool down. She should have recognized then that things weren't fantastic between them. He'd tried a third time and after he popped the first button off her blouse, Polly asked him to stop. When he didn't, she grabbed his wrist, turned it around to his back and pushed him face first into the sofa. He never tried that move again.

He'd also been wonderful to her about that, too, even when she felt guilty because she'd gotten so aggressive. But now that she thought about, she grew furious. He'd been the aggressor that evening and she protected herself. Why the heck did she feel guilty about stopping him? Why? Because Joey told her that it was okay she'd gotten aggressive with him.

Polly looked down at her lap and slowly unclenched her fingers from around the bouquet of roses; thankful for the many layers of paper protecting her fingers from the bite of thorns.

Joey had really done a number on her. What the heck was up with her thinking she wasn't ladylike because she'd chosen to take him down? She chuckled and gave her head a quick shake. For the most part, Joey was a gentleman, and after their third wrestling match, he backed way off. He was gentle with her, never pushing more than she wanted. She knew that if their physical relationship was going any deeper, she'd have to be the one to initiate things. It was hard to believe that she'd never been interested in him that way. Joey wanted to marry her and yet she couldn't bear the thought of being physically intimate with him. Yeah. It was a good idea for them to break up. She should have realized that earlier. At least then she wouldn't have to avoid her favorite cafe or wonder if she was going to be sued by some poor guy who simply wanted to thank her for a book recommendation. What a mess she'd gotten herself into simply because she hadn't recognized that she'd rather be alone than with Joey.

The whole mess with court and jail had been her undoing. Polly was pretty sure that was the point when Joey's obsession with her grew out of control. No one else in his life wanted anything to do with him. That should also have been a clue. She felt sorry for him and her protective instincts kicked in. If his family wasn't going to be there for him, then she would take their place.

Polly huffed. What a fool she'd been.

"Ready for the season to start?"

"Yes?" Polly asked. "What season?"

"This is the year for the Sox, don't you think?"

"Oh yeah," Polly said with a laugh. "It has to happen soon, that's for sure."

"What do you think about Padilla being signed?"

Polly bit her lip. She had absolutely no idea who the woman was talking about. She enjoyed watching baseball and had been to a few games, but evidently, she had missed out on some pertinent information. "I don't actually know."

"Yeah. None of us do. I hope it's a good match. A lot of injuries, but we're holding out hope."

The car came to a stop in front of the library and Polly handed over her credit card and swiped a tip. "Thank you," Polly said.

"Have a good day and take care of those pretty roses. Somebody loves you."

Polly took a rose from the bouquet and held it across the seat. "This is for you. I hope you have a fantastic day."

"Thank you, Miss," the woman said. "That's sweet. You sure you won't miss it?"

"I have quite a few more. One won't be missed." Polly got out of the car and after closing the door, stepped up onto the sidewalk. She took a deep breath and looked around, hoping the shiver that went down her back was from the chill in the air and nothing else. She didn't see anything out of place and headed inside, smiling at people as she passed by them. The only way she was getting through this day was by grit and determination. Joey wasn't allowed to destroy her day, no matter what. She had to manage her way through it.

"Whoa, lookie those," Janet said, when Polly crossed behind the counter. "From your sweetie? He's so nice. I wish I had a boyfriend like Joey Delancy. I'd never let him go."

Polly bit her lip. The little dimwit had no idea what reality looked like. "Do you think there's a vase around? More people could enjoy them here. They'd just go to waste at my place."

Janet jumped off the stool she'd been sitting on. "I know where there's one." She put her hands out. "Let me take them. My mother always told me that I had a talent with flowers. I'll arrange them and everything." She peered into the bouquet and then ran her finger around the blossoms, counting. "There's only eleven. What's up with that?"

"I gave one to the taxi driver. She seemed like she needed a flower today." Polly put the bouquet into Janet's hands and reached into her pocket. Pulling out her wallet, she took out ten dollars. "I'm sorry about lunch yesterday. I hope you were okay."

"Yeah. Ilsa got the call from Mrs. Gavin that you weren't coming back. She said you got sick. You didn't look sick when you left. Did you and Joey have a nooner or something?"

Polly gritted her teeth. "No. Nothing like that. Something came on me really hard at lunch and there was no way I could stay here all afternoon." She handed the ten-dollar bill to Janet. "I'm sorry I messed your lunch up."

"That's okay. Like I said, Ilsa got the call and I figured you weren't bringing me anything, so we had lunch delivered. It was nice."

"I'm glad." Polly took her jacket off. They didn't have much time before the doors opened to the public and there was a lot of work that needed to be done first. "You go take care of the roses and I'll start on these books."

CHAPTER FIVE

Mid-February

"I'm worried about you. You look like hell." Sal took Polly's arm as they walked down Boylston Street. "What's going on?"

Polly shook her head. "Nothing."

Sal turned her into The Lenox. "We're drinking tonight. If I have to put you in a cab, I will."

"I still have to go to work in the morning," Polly said. "And so do you."

"We're young and I don't care." Sal motioned for Polly to precede her into the hotel and then led her to the bar.

Dim lighting, crushed velvet seating, and a bustling crowd of people finished with work for the day seemed like the right place to finally have this conversation with Sal. Polly had been avoiding her friends since the breakup. She just hadn't been prepared to discuss it with them.

Polly came to a full stop and looked out over the crowded room.

"Come on." Sal took her hand and they wove their way in and

around people until she put her hand on the back of a chair. "Sit. I need to go to the bathroom. If a waiter shows up, order appetizers and a Cosmo for me."

Polly sat and picked up the menu, a little stunned. But this was Sal. Always in charge and always moving. Polly preferred the suburbs, but Sal loved the insanity of downtown. The funny thing was that Sal worked and lived out in the suburbs, while Polly worked downtown.

"May I help you this evening?" A young man stopped in front of Polly. "Oh my," he said. "You need a drink."

Polly sat back. "Do I look that bad?"

"Your eyes look sad." He smiled. "And a little stressed out. How about this one?" He pointed at an item on the cocktail menu.

"Gin, lemon juice and champagne." Polly smiled up at him. "That sounds amazing. My friend wants a Cosmopolitan."

He moved his finger up the page. "We have a blood orange Cosmo or I can ask the bartender to make something a tad more boring."

"Sal is not boring," Polly said. "The blood orange will be perfect and we'll start with the house made potato chips."

"Are you sure that's all you want to start with?"

She giggled. "Do I want something else?"

"I believe you might enjoy the Margherita Pizza as well. Then, something simple like our lobster bisque and a chopped salad for dinner." He waggled his eyebrows at her. "How am I doing?"

Polly put the menu back on the table. "You know your customers, don't you?"

"My name is Philippe. If there is anything else that you need this evening, don't hesitate to stand up and wave for me. I'll be here immediately."

Sal slid into the chair across from Polly.

"You're the other beautiful woman in this party?" Philippe asked. "I should have known. You are a perfect blood orange Cosmo."

He turned and walked away, leaving Sal with her mouth open. "What was that?"

"That was Philippe. He seems to know what we need to drink and eat tonight."

"Oh he does, does he? We'll see about that. What did you get for appetizers?"

"I was just going for some of their homemade potato chips, but he said we needed the Margherita pizza, too."

Sal looked down and read the description. "That sounds amazing. But what if we want supper?"

"Apparently I'm having lobster bisque and a chopped salad."

"What a great idea. I wonder if that's what I'm having." Sal let out a cackle. "I love this city." She reached across the table and took Polly's hand. "What's going on with you? I haven't seen you online. I haven't heard from you and you didn't sound exactly thrilled when I called about going out tonight."

"It's a lot of things," Polly said. She picked the menu back up.

"No you don't." Sal pushed it back to the table. "Talk to me. Is it Joey?"

Polly let out a long breath. "We broke up."

"Thank goodness," Sal said. She gave her head a quick shake. "That wasn't nice of me. Do you miss him? When did it happen? Who broke up with who? Are you sad?"

"Not really sad at all. It's been two weeks. I'm actually more freaked out than I am sad."

"Freaked out? What does that mean?" Sal leaned forward, her eyebrows furrowed. "Is he threatening you? I can totally see him doing that. Tell me everything. Start at the beginning. What happened two weeks ago to make you break up with him?"

"He attacked another man," Polly said. "Just a guy who talked to me in the library. You know? At my job? Joey was in the library that day spying on me. He walked out with the guy, threw him up against the building and started yelling at him. I had to pull Joey off." She shook her head and gulped. "It was so embarrassing. If it had gone on for another minute, security would have been there and Joey would have been taken away again. As it is I can't believe that guy didn't try to sue me or the library."

"Sue you?"

Polly shook her head. "No. He wouldn't have done that. I'm being dramatic. We went to the cafe and Joey just didn't get any more normal. Then he told me that he stopped going to those anger management classes and wasn't seeing the counselor any longer. It hit me that he just plain disgusted me, so I left the cafe and went home. I changed my locks and changed my phone number."

"Yeah," Sal said. "That was weird. Good thing I could reach you at work. I just figured ..." She huffed. "I don't know what I figured, but I sure didn't think it had anything to do with Joey. Has he tried to get back in touch with you?"

Philippe stepped back up to their table and placed the two drinks down. "Ladies," he said with a smile. "I will be back with your appetizers in just a few minutes. My prediction is that you will each desire at least one, if not two more of these wonderful drinks before you leave this evening. All you have to do is to wave at me and I will start their preparation at once." He stepped back and Sal looked up at him with a grin. "Go ahead." With a grand flourish, he gestured at the drinks. "Taste them before I depart from your presence. I want to be certain that you are as happy as I can make you."

Polly laughed until she snorted, then covered her mouth with her hand. This young man was getting a big tip tonight.

Sal took a sip of her drink and licked her lips before taking a bigger drink. "You might as well start my second one right now," she said. "I'm in love."

"Of that I am certain," Philippe responded. He turned to Polly. "Now, it is your turn. Tell me that I am correct about what thrills your taste buds. Make me feel like a winner."

She could barely contain her laughter, but brought the drink to her mouth and sipped it.

"Oh no, you must take in more than that," he said. "Trust me."

She took a longer drink. He was right. The champagne tickled her nose and the gin and lemon were mixed in perfect proportions. "It's perfection." Polly kissed her fingertips and extended her fingers. "Pure perfection."

"But of course. Will one be enough?"

Polly shook her head. "If you're bringing back a second for my friend, bring mine as well."

"Let Philippe care for you this fine evening. He knows what beautiful women need."

After he walked away, Sal took two audible breaths. "Apparently I need me some of that. Oh. My. God."

"I know," Polly said, letting out a laugh. "I'm about to embarrass myself."

They took several more sips in silence. Polly couldn't believe she was shamelessly flirting with a young man she'd never see again in her life.

Sal shook her head as if shaking off a trance. "Whew. I need to stop objectifying that young man."

"I suspect he likes it," Polly replied. "He's playing the game as hard as anyone I've ever seen."

"Let's get back to Joey."

Polly shook her head. "Let's not. This is more fun."

"So you broke up with him, changed your locks and your phone number. Have you seen him since? I'm surprised he hasn't been knocking at your door."

"I was worried about that. I finally convinced myself that I'd call the police if he showed up." Polly scowled. "Even though he hasn't shown up at my door, I'm pretty sure he's been hanging around. The first morning I came out to roses on my doorstep and then there have been the letters." She rolled her eyes. "Oh, the letters - long, handwritten pieces of prose confessing his undying love for me, his sorrow at the terrible crime against me he committed, and how we should be together."

"Have you kept them?"

"No. They're disgusting."

"Disgusting, disgusting?"

"Not like that. He'd never write that in a letter. No, it's just all gooey, lovey-dovey stuff about how he can't live without seeing the sunshine light up my eyes or feeling the warmth of my hand in his. That kind of disgusting."

"And you get these in the mail?"

This was what Polly didn't want to admit. She took another delightful drink and steeled herself. "Sometimes they come through the mail. But sometimes they are under the wipers of my car or tucked into my doorway."

"Polly Giller, you have to call the police," Sal said, putting her empty glass down hard on the table. "This guy is dangerous. He's stalking you. Tell me you're smart enough to make sure your drapes are always closed."

"Of course they are. But the thing is, if they're closed that means I can't see out. I feel like he's always there, but of course I have no proof."

"Other than letters showing up where there should be no letters. If you don't call the police, then at least call your friend, Drea. She's got a couple of brothers who would deal with him. Ask them for help."

"No," Polly said quietly. "I'm not asking the Renaldi brothers to step into this one. I don't want them getting into trouble because of Joey. They'd do something stupid and he'd end up in the Charles."

"It would serve him right." Sal glared at Polly. "I suspect they could make sure his body was never found."

Polly laughed. "I'm not involving them in this. I can handle Joey."

"Really?" Sal pointed at Polly. "You look exhausted. You aren't sleeping, are you?"

Polly shrugged.

"And I'll bet you aren't eating either. I swear, you've lost ten pounds since the last time I saw you. Your eyes are all sunken in and you've got terrible bags. If you weren't wearing makeup, I'd probably see dark circles. Am I right?"

"I'm not wearing makeup, Sal. And thanks for telling me how pretty I look this evening. You really know how to make a girl feel good."

"Well, I'm sorry, but you are a mess. And it's all because of that damned jackass. It was bad enough when you put up with his idiotic behavior because you thought you liked him. Now you're putting up with his crap and you know better."

"He'll move on. It's only been a couple of weeks. Once he realizes this isn't going to actually go anywhere, he'll find someone else."

"Tell me you haven't responded to any of his letters."

Polly looked at her in shock. "Uh. No. That would be stupid. He doesn't care if he gets negative or positive feedback, any of that would encourage him. I refuse to do that."

"At least you're that smart." Sal smiled. "Oh look. Philippe is back. Drink up. That's a good girl, you can do it."

"All of it?" Polly hadn't been quite as attentive to her drink.

"All of it. We don't want to make him wait to take away your empty, now do we?"

"Of course not." Polly took three long drinks, finishing as Philippe swept in to their table.

He smiled at her and Polly's eyes grew big. "You're very pretty," she said and giggled. "I need food."

"You aren't wrong, though," Sal said. She batted her eyes at Philippe as he put another Cosmo in front of her and removed her empty glass. "I could take you home to mother."

"Now you girls are getting into the spirit of things," Philippe said. He replaced Polly's drink and put a plate in front of each of them. "Here are your chips and the pizza. Allow these to absorb some of the alcohol so that you can stay and enjoy yourselves. I will be back in just a bit to check on you."

"You don't happen to have a couple of glasses of water in your back pocket, do you?" Polly asked.

"Not in my back pocket," Philippe said, "but right over your head." He produced two glasses of water from behind Polly.

When she turned around, she realized that the back of her seat was up against a counter. "Oh, and here I thought you were magic."

"My dear, there are many things about me which are magical. Remember, if you need anything, just wave and I'll be in front of you before your next heartbeat."

"He has to be taken," Polly said, leaning across the table so she could speak low enough he wouldn't hear.

"That would just figure. I swear," Sal said, "I'm so tired of blind dates and lousy men. If my mother sets me up with one more son of a friend of a friend, I'm going to scream. I don't like any of those men. They are all so vapid."

"Vapid?" Polly giggled. "That's a great word. Come on, your mother wouldn't do that to you."

Sal gave her a look. "You've met the woman, haven't you? She doesn't care who I marry, just that he has money and connections and keeps me occupied so I don't let the world know I actually have a brain. Us JAPs can't have brains, you know."

"You be nice," Polly said.

"Not gonna. I'm getting a happy little buzz. I'm mad at you and I'm mad at Joey and now I'm mad at my mother."

"Why are you mad at me?"

"Because it took you two weeks to tell me what was going on. You've been living with this all by yourself. Have you told anyone else?"

Polly shook her head. "Who am I going to tell? And besides, it's my fault. I need to figure it out and deal with it."

"But you aren't dealing with it. You're hiding in your house not eating and not sleeping. That's not healthy and it's not dealing with it."

"I just need some time. It's going to work out. You'll see." Polly sighed and then took a long drink. This was exactly what she needed.

CHAPTER SIX

Late February

No amount of caffeine helped her get through these long days. Polly yawned as she dropped her coat on a chair in the staff room and sat down. This not sleeping stuff was killing her. Joey should have moved on, but she'd gotten another long letter from him last night. It had been tucked into a gift bag filled with chocolates and the entire set of Harry Potter novels, because she'd once lamented that her copies were packed in boxes back in Iowa. He was never going to leave her alone - his letters became more and more insistent. His desperation over losing her was ridiculous. He hadn't crossed a line yet, but Polly had no idea when that might happen. He hadn't hurt her, he hadn't threatened her, and he had never even approached or harassed her. He was just there all the time. She thought about moving. There was so much money sitting in that trust back in Iowa. She could afford to buy a home, though prices in the Boston area were just plain out of sight.

She rejected the idea of moving. She wasn't ready for that kind of a commitment here. In her gut, Polly knew that wouldn't do any good anyway. Joey would find a way to track her down no matter where she lived. She needed to get far away from him.

"Polly?"

She looked up to see Mrs. Gavin's secretary, Louise, standing over her. She sat up and brushed her hair away from her eyes. "I'm sorry. I got lost in thought. I need to clock in."

"No," Louise said, smiling at her. "That's not why I'm here. Go ahead and clock in, but Mrs. Gavin would like to see you when you have a few minutes. She's free right now."

"Have I done something?" Polly stood up.

"You're fine. She'd just like a few minutes of your time. Come on up. I have good coffee in the office if you'd like that."

Polly chuckled, a bit with relief and a bit at the idea of drinking good coffee. With all the coffee shops around, she'd grown used to the good stuff. At home, Mary and Polly's dad drank nothing but Folgers. Until Polly got to college she had no idea that coffee could be such an extraordinary treat. "I'll be right up."

"Take your time." Louise left the room. The woman was quite motherly, actually grand-motherly. She wore smart, sharp suits, but her gray hair was always pulled into a loose bun at the back of her head and she wore just enough lipstick to let you know that she had some on, but never too much. Louise baked and was forever bringing in cookies and brownies. People did almost anything to visit Mrs. Gavin. Polly was pretty sure that Louise did it on purpose so she had plenty of company.

Polly clocked in, put her coat away and went upstairs, arriving just as Louise took her seat.

"That was fast," Louise said, standing back up. "Come on in. I'll bring coffee to you. Blueberry muffins are already in there." She held the door open to Mrs. Gavin's office and waited for Polly to pass through.

"Thank you," Polly said. Nerves hit her stomach as soon as she crossed the threshold. Her boss was a very nice person, but Polly was rarely called into her office.

Mrs. Gavin reminded Polly of Ruth Bader Ginsburg. She was a petite woman with severe features. Just as you grew accustomed to the fact that she might never smile, one broke out and the room lit up.

"Hello, Polly." Mrs. Gavin pulled a chair out at the small conference table and gestured to it. "Please come in and have a seat. Louise's blueberry muffins are wonderful this morning. They were still warm when she brought them in." She looked up when the door opened. "And here's your coffee."

Louise placed the coffee cup on the table and then closed the door before returning to sit with Polly and Mrs. Gavin. "Go ahead, dear," Louise said, taking up the platter of muffins. She removed one to a small plate in front of her and passed the platter to Polly.

Since it seemed that taking a muffin was expected, Polly followed suit and passed the platter to Mrs. Gavin, who put it back in the center of the table.

"How are you doing, Polly?" Mrs. Gavin asked.

"I'm doing okay. Winter is wearing me out. This has been a long one so far."

Mrs. Gavin gave a slight chuckle. "It has definitely taken its toll on us. My poor pups despise going outside. I must confess that my husband has scooped snow from a portion of the lawn so they have a place to go to the bathroom. They refuse to plant those delicate little feet of theirs in the cold, wet snow." She turned to Louise. "Please don't tell Polly how spoiled they are. It might ruin my image."

Louise clamped her lips between a thumb and forefinger. "My lips are sealed."

"Are you happy here, Polly?" Mrs. Gavin asked.

Startled at such a direct question, Polly glanced at Louise, then back at Mrs. Gavin. "Of course I am. I love it here. My entire life has led me to this. I'm so lucky to have this job."

"And your co-workers? Do you spend much time with any of them outside of work?"

Polly shook her head. She had no idea what was going on. "Not really. I have a few friends that I do things with, but no one from here."

"But you get along with them okay?"

Other than Janet? That girl drove Polly batty. She kept that all inside her head and said, "Absolutely. We enjoy working together. At least I do. Is there a problem?"

Mrs. Gavin shook her head. "No. Not at all. But I must confess that I'm worried about you."

"Worried about me? Have I done something? Or not done something?"

"Oh," Mrs. Gavin said, putting her hand on top of Polly's. "No. Not at all. This isn't a performance review. If it were, yours would be excellent. That's not what this is at all." The woman took a breath, as if she were trying to decide what to say next. "In the last few months, Polly, you have lost weight. Are you on a special diet? Is there something physically wrong with you?"

Polly shook her head and looked at the table. "No. I'm healthy. And I'm not on a diet."

"Good. Because you certainly didn't need to be. I wouldn't have said anything, but you've lost something else."

"Your spark, honey," Louise interjected. "You've lost your happiness. You don't smile easily any more. You always seem to be looking over your shoulder. While you're doing your job quite well, it's become nothing more than a job for you. When you first came to work here, you practically flew through the stacks - like you were dancing among the books. When you were working, everyone was happy. And my dear, patrons have also asked if you're okay. Mr. Stringer found his way up here to talk to us about you the other day. He's worried."

Mr. Stringer was one of Polly's special patrons. He'd come out of his shell during the years they worked together. Nobody else wanted to spend time helping the man. Ilsa just plain ignored him whenever he came up for assistance. Polly had gotten to know him and discovered he had a wry sense of humor, but was terrified of interacting with people, so he came off as gruff and angry. That he went out of his way to speak to her boss was a big deal.

"I'm sorry," Polly said quietly.

"We aren't looking for an apology," Mrs. Gavin said. "But if there is something happening in your life and I can help you with it, I'd like to do that. You're one of my favorite people and I hate that you might be hurting. Has someone hurt you?"

Polly felt tears threaten and she looked down, gulping to keep them back. "Not really. No. I'm sorry, though. I'll try to shake this off. I understand what you're saying to me."

"This isn't a criticism, dear," Louise said. "We're worried about you. What can we do to help?"

"There's really nothing. I just need to get through it."

Mrs. Gavin gave Polly's hand a squeeze. "Polly, you weren't in this bad of shape when your father died or when your friend, Mary, died. Maybe you need to talk to someone. We miss you."

Taking a long, deep breath, Polly nodded. "I will see what I can do to manage this. I didn't realize it was so noticeable."

"Honey, why don't you take the rest of the day off. Go stand in front of the ocean. Find a quiet spot. Let peace find its way back into your soul. Think about what it is that you need to do to reclaim yourself. We will support you in any decision that you make."

"I can work today," Polly protested.

"Of course you can," Mrs. Gavin said. "But I'm giving you a free day off. Take it. Refresh yourself. If you need to take tomorrow off, do that. Drive down the coast. The weather has given us a break and you should take advantage of it. Give yourself some freedom. Then come back to us."

"Are you sure?" Polly was flabbergasted at this behavior, but she'd been here long enough to know that Mrs. Gavin ran her department better than most. She paid attention to her employees.

"We're sure." Louise stood and left the office, surprising both Polly and Mrs. Gavin.

"Quite sure," Mrs. Gavin said, glancing at the door. "You need to deal with whatever is bothering you because right now it's destroying you."

"I'm so sorry that I let it take over my work," Polly said. "I didn't mean to do that."

"I understand."

Louise came back in with a lid for the coffee cup she'd placed in front of Polly. She shook out a small paper sack and filled it with the rest of the muffins from the plate. "Take these with you. There's nothing like some homemade muffins to make a girl feel better. They'll be perfect for a drive down the coast."

Polly smiled and stood. "Thank you both," she said. "I will work this out."

"Call me tomorrow," Mrs. Gavin said, putting out her hand.

When Polly reached out to shake it, Mrs. Gavin took Polly's in both of hers and gripped it firmly. "Take care of yourself. We want you around for a very long time."

Polly went back downstairs and into the staff bathroom. She stood in front of the sink and looked in the mirror. What she saw shocked her. They were right. She'd lost weight. She hadn't even realized how much. Mary would be so worried. There was nothing left to her cheeks. Her eyes were dark and when she attempted to smile, it was nothing like what she was used to seeing. Polly made an attempt to fluff her hair. It hadn't been cut in months and hung limply around her face. The sheen and luster was gone. She was a wreck. She'd known that her clothes were loose, but when Polly looked down, she realized the dress she was wearing looked like a sack.

When was the last time she'd even looked in a mirror? Really looked. She couldn't remember. When she brushed her teeth in the morning, she'd quit bothering to wipe the steam away. All she did was pull a comb through her wet hair and get dressed. This was what her coworkers were seeing. Polly couldn't imagine what Drea or Sal, or even Bunny, would say to her. She hadn't seen any of them in such a long time. The last time she saw Sal was when they'd had that wonderful evening at The Lenox. Bunny had been so caught up in whatever new boy she was dating that she spent just long enough on the phone with Polly to talk about her own life. She never asked questions about what was happening with Polly. And that was perfectly fine. That was who Bunny was.

Sal and Drea each called a couple of times, but Polly had

pushed them off, assuring them she was fine, but busy. Busy. Hah. She did nothing but work and sit at home either reading or watching television.

Polly couldn't remember the last time she'd cooked a decent meal for supper either. She usually got a sandwich at lunch and then ate a couple of pieces of toast before bed if she was hungry. She wasn't hungry very often. This was craziness. Joey had her so messed up that she was wrecking her life. If Mr. Springer noticed and actually spoke to her boss, that was bad. It was time to do something else. Anything else. She couldn't keep doing this.

Three raps at the door preceded Janet's voice. "Polly, you okay in there?"

"I'll be right out." Polly pushed her hair away from her face, then tucked it behind her ear. Yeah. She really needed to make new decisions. He didn't get to control her life. That was something only she got to do.

"You okay?" Janet asked when Polly exited the bathroom. "Mrs. Gavin said you're going home. Are you sick? Do you want me to call someone? I could call that nice guy you dated. What was his name?"

"No," Polly replied. "You don't need to call anyone. I've got this. But I am going home. I need to work a few things out."

"Like what?"

"Like things. *My* things." Polly pushed past the girl and grabbed up her coat.

"I'd be glad to talk to you if you need an ear."

Polly had her back to Janet, so she allowed herself to close her eyes and breathe, ensuring that the next words out of her mouth wouldn't be exceptionally rude. "No. Thank you. I've got this, but I appreciate your concern."

"Well, any time. I'm always here for you if you need a friend."

Polly picked up the bag of muffins and her coffee, then turned to smile at Janet. "Thank you. I'll talk to you later."

"What should I tell your boyfriend when he comes in looking for you?"

Polly stopped. "He comes in looking for me?"

"I've seen him a couple of times." Janet shrugged. "He looks around and then he leaves."

"Don't tell him anything," Polly said. "If he needs to know something about me, it's my job to tell him, not yours."

"Whatever," Janet said. "Just trying to be helpful."

Polly left the room and muttered under her breath, "It's your best thing."

CHAPTER SEVEN

Ever since Janet started working at the library, she'd been a thorn in Polly's side. It was time to let that go. There were too many other things to consider.

Polly got in her car and took a long, deep breath. What a strange morning. She didn't feel like driving down the coast and she wasn't going home. Her apartment felt like a cell. Instead, she drove along the Charles River, smiling as she passed the outskirts of Harvard University. Seriously. Here she was, driving past like it was no big deal. She'd gotten used to the history over the years. Places that had been nothing more than locations on a map or sites in a story, were now as commonplace as the back yard of her old house. She meandered through Cambridge and realized that she knew exactly where she was going. It wasn't someplace that many people went, but on one visit her father asked to see the place where Winslow Homer painted *Boys in a Pasture*. They'd seen the painting at the Museum of Fine Arts and something in it affected him. He'd talked about growing up with his brother, Clyde, and sitting out in a field looking up at the clouds in the sky.

Belmont was a nice community and there was still plenty of wooded area just north of Concord Avenue. Nice community. Whatever. It was a very wealthy community. Lots of old money in there. Sal told stories of rich girls she'd known from Belmont. But still, today wasn't about that.

She wound her way through town and found Somerset Street and the open field across from an elegant old home. Some of it was taken up with tennis courts, but it was too cold for anyone to be playing. Polly pulled into a parking spot and turned the heat up. She needed to think. What she really needed was to talk to her father. He'd listen to her fears and then ask what it was she really wanted from life. Polly couldn't answer that today. It felt like everything was pressing in on her.

"I miss you, Dad," she said. "I really miss you today. I don't want to do this anymore. I don't want to live like this. I'm tired of it. I'm tired of it all."

Polly could almost hear him respond. "Are you just reacting to your worry about Joey? Or are you truly tired of living out here so far from everything you grew up with?"

"It's really different, Dad, but we talked about that. People in the city are a far cry from those I grew up with. They're all so busy. I'm busy." She huffed. "That's not true. I'm not busy at all. Dad, I get tired of long drives to work and that crazy traffic. The other morning some guy completely blocked traffic so he could rescue a dog who'd gotten into the middle of the traffic circle. People were pissed off - screaming at him, honking their horns. I don't know if I could have done that. He acted like he didn't care about the noise. I would have cared. How wrong is that? I'm not that person."

"Are you happy out here, Polly?" he would have asked.

She grimaced. "I'm not sure if I even know what that means. A few months ago, I would have said yes. It scares me to think that I'm allowing Joey to color my emotions like this, but Dad, I don't think so. I have fun with my friends when I'm with them and I really like my job, but that's it. I have nothing else in my life - just a few friends and my job. What kind of life is that? You had a whole town that liked you. And your Christmas kids? Every time you showed up with a bag filled with toys, they went crazy. You knew you were doing something good. I'm not doing anything good out here. I'm not doing anything. Am I crazy to believe that I should have more than this in my life?" She shook her head and sipped from the coffee cup Louise had given her. The coffee was lukewarm, but it was still really good coffee.

Everett would have given her his all-knowing smile. "You know that you should have more than this in your life. You deserve everything. You're my daughter and I love you. The sky is the limit."

"I love you, too, Dad," Polly said quietly. "I was never going to marry Joey, but he was fun for a while. I guess I always thought that someday I'd meet some great guy and marry him. We'd live in a small community. Maybe not Belmont, but something around here."

Maybe even up in Medford so she could be close to the Renaldis. That would be a riot. No, it was probably a bad idea. Mama Renaldi would decide Polly needed to be reined in. However, she'd get to know more people. That would be great. Polly needed more people in her life.

"What am I doing, Dad? If I don't want to live here, where do I want to live?"

One word came into her head. "Home."

As soon as she heard the words, tears flowed down her cheeks. She missed home. Not just her dad and Mary, but home. She missed big wide-open spaces. She missed knowing nearly everyone in town and smiling at them when she walked into a shop. She missed the one-finger wave out on country roads and the quiet. Wow, she missed the quiet.

Polly tilted the rear-view mirror down so she could look at herself. "You have to get rid of that sunken-face thing, Polly Giller. Living is too important and you aren't really living out here. You're existing. Just because you have a job that matches your degree doesn't mean that is your life. If you want to work in a library, go home and find a job in a small town. They'd love to have you. Or don't. You have plenty of money waiting for you to do something with it. That investment has been growing. Quit acting like you shouldn't touch it. It's yours. All yours. Live a little. Travel."

She chuckled. Travel was fun, but not her thing. Bunny loved to travel. She would get on a flight going nearly anywhere if someone paid for it. Now, the girl would carry her entire wardrobe, plus every stinking thing in her bathroom, but she loved going places.

No. Traveling wasn't for Polly, but she didn't need to waste away any longer. She needed to make changes and she needed to do it right now before she lost her nerve.

Taking another drink of her coffee, Polly put it back into the cup holder, backed out of the parking space and headed for home. She needed to make a call. There was no reason to go back to work. She didn't need that job. She'd saved so much money over the years that she could live quite well for a couple of years without working if she wanted to. But it wasn't going to take that long. Something was going to happen. Polly reached into the bag of muffins and took one out. She stopped at the entrance to Concord Avenue and unwrapped the muffin, then took a bite. Moaning, she took another. Louise certainly could bake. This was amazing. She hadn't tasted something so wonderful in months.

Her stomach growled as she passed a fast food joint so she turned in and went through the drive-through, ordering a burger and fries as well as another coffee. Was that really all it took? She was starving. By the time Polly got home, she'd finished the sandwich and fries and had eaten another muffin. Grabbing up the trash, she locked her car and went inside. She threw open the curtains and looked around. The place was a disaster. She'd been living on the couch for so long it was completely misshapen.

Polly puffed up the cushions on the couch and opened her laptop. She hadn't even been on social media for a few weeks, always worried that Joey would stalk her there. At this point, she didn't give a damn. She could block him, ignore him, and make him go away.

She swiped her phone open and looked through the contacts. Steve Cook had worked with her dad for years and now took care of Polly's investments. He'd talk to her. She steeled herself and made the call.

"Cook and Hodgkins," a voice answered. "How may I help you?"

"Hi. This is Polly Giller. Is Steve around?"

"Hello, Miss Giller. He sure is. Hold on just a minute."

It didn't take long before Steve's calm voice was there. "Polly. How are you?"

"I'm good. Do you have a few minutes?"

"Sure I do. What's up?"

"I want to come back to Iowa. I'm ready to do something very different."

He chuckled. "That sounds like a big decision. What do you want to do and how can I help?"

"I don't know the answer to either of those questions yet. I just know that I'm ready to do something with that chunk of money that's sitting there wasting away."

"It's been doing pretty good lately," Steve said. "No wasting away as far as I can tell. What are you thinking?"

Polly shut her eyes. "I'm not sure yet, but I want to move back to a small town where I can get to know people."

"You thinking Story City?"

"No!" That came out faster and louder than she expected. "Sorry. No, I don't want to come back to Dad's town. I want something else. I'd like to stay in the Ames area since I know that pretty well. What kind of thing would make sense for me?"

"Do you want to invest in land?"

"Yeah. That sounds right. Something that I can bring back to life. An old church. Someplace I can live, but I want to re-build it so that the community would have a reason to be there. If I did an old church, maybe we could turn part of it into classrooms where there would be lessons - music lessons or knitting lessons. You remember how Mrs. Schiff had that craft store downtown? I tried to learn how to knit from her. It was a bad idea, but I tried. Little towns don't get to have those kinds of things anymore because everybody heads out to the big box stores. Or maybe I'd sell antiques - anything to get involved with the town. I know I'm crazy, but it feels like restoring an old building is the right thing to do."

As soon as the words were out of her mouth, Polly realized that was exactly what she was looking for. She needed to bring something back to life.

"That's kind of a tall order," Steve said.

"I can afford it, though, right?"

"Well. Yes."

"What does that mean?"

"It doesn't really mean anything. If we can get a good deal on a building, you need to hire a contractor. You don't want to do the work yourself, do you?"

"I'll do anything that I can," she said. "I can paint. I can learn how to run a saw. If I have to climb up on a roof and put shingles down, I'll do it." She chuckled. "I'll dig dirt, I'll do anything. But I need life to be real again."

"Construction and renovation is about as real as you can get. When do you want to get started? Are you talking about six months? Next year?"

"Next week," Polly said. "I'm quitting my job tomorrow and then I'm packing everything up and heading for Iowa."

He laughed. "You and your Dad are two peas in a pod. Once you get something in your head, you go forward with barely a glance back. You're sure about this?"

"I couldn't be more sure," Polly said. "What do I need to do next?"

"Tell you what. Let me do some checking. I have a couple of friends in real estate. If there's anything in the area, they'll know where it is. Can I slow you down at all?"

"Nope. I'm ready to get moving. It will take time for me to wrap things up here, but while I'm doing that, I want you to move forward." She took a breath. "Dad wouldn't hate this idea, would he?"

"No Polly. He'd support whatever you want to do. We're going to want to sit down, though, and draw up a good plan for going forward unless you just want to renovate an old house for yourself to live in."

Polly thought about that for a moment. "Not yet. I want something more than that. When I'm finished I want to add to whatever community I'm living in. I want to do something important with this money."

"Then I'll make some calls. Why don't you give me until the end of the week?"

"Send me an email when you have some ideas. Then we can talk again."

"You're really just moving back here like that? Have you not been happy out there? The last we talked, I thought you enjoyed your job."

"My job is terrific, but it hit me today that all I have is my job and a few friends. I don't really have a life. I know that I could change things and find a way to create a life, but wow, it's been fourteen years and nothing's all that much different than when I moved here. That's a long time to be in limbo."

"Yes it is. Well, let me see what I can track down. If you have any other ideas, don't hesitate to reach out."

"Thank you, Steve."

When she put her phone back on the coffee table, Polly felt lighter than she had in months. For that matter, years.

"Okay, house. We're cleaning you today." She went into the kitchen and took out a box of garbage bags. The first thing that needed to happen was a purge. Her spice cabinet was a good place to begin. Polly opened it and laughed at the ridiculous amount of spices on the shelves. Ten years of accumulation; some she hadn't touched since the day she purchased them.

Mrs. Gavin was going to be quite surprised at Polly's decision.

No. That probably wasn't true. Mrs. Gavin had known that something big needed to change in Polly's life.

Sal, Drea, and Bunny were going to be surprised. They were used to having her around all the time. She was used to having them around. But things were going to be different now. Polly was changing everything. She'd miss her friends, but that was okay. They'd always stay in touch.

Polly lifted up on her tip toes and twirled around. "It's all going to change," she said.

CHAPTER EIGHT

Smiling when she saw Bunny Farnam's picture pop up on her phone, Polly swiped the call open. "Good morning, sweet pea."

"What are you doing today?" Bunny asked. "We have to go shopping. Please say yes. Please, please, please, please, please."

"Yes?"

"You will?"

"What are we shopping for?"

"I don't know. I didn't expect you to say yes. You're always so busy."

"I'm not busy today." That really wasn't true. Polly was packing like a wild woman. After giving her notice at the library, the last two weeks had flown by. Mrs. Gavin accepted Polly's resignation and told her that she was happy to hear that she'd made a positive decision. Yesterday was her good-bye lunch. Polly had worried there might be tears ... on her part, but no, she was ready to go. This weekend was going to be the tough part. She hadn't told any of her friends yet that she was leaving Boston.

Drea had been out of the country, so Polly didn't feel terribly guilty about that, but Sal? Well, Polly was terrified of what her friend would say. They'd not seen too much of each other lately, but that wasn't abnormal. They both had busy lives and Boston was a big city. And then there was the fact that Polly was avoiding the conversation.

"If you aren't busy today," Bunny said, "then let's do something wild. Where shall we go?"

Bunny's idea of something wild was spending enormous amounts of time in expensive boutiques, trying on the latest in high fashion. Sal didn't understand why Polly and Bunny were friends. She could barely stand the girl, but for some reason, Polly just loved the self-centered dingbat, though generally only in small doses.

"I tell you what. Why don't we start at Neiman Marcus," Polly said.

"That's boring. Everybody shops there. I want to go to Chanel."

Polly burst out laughing. "I can't afford Chanel and neither can you."

"But I can dream. Come dream with me."

Right across from Boston Public Gardens, Chanel was just the beginning of upscale shops Bunny would try to drag Polly to. This had happened several times in the past, but it had been a few years, so Polly was probably due. She always felt dowdy in those stores, no matter how she dressed.

"Let's have breakfast first," Polly said. "Or lunch. There's something I want to tell you."

"Are you and that Joey finally getting married?" Bunny asked. "I can't wait to get married. I keep hoping my prince will arrive, but so far, no such luck. Would you believe that I went out on a date with a twenty-five-year-old last week? He was a child. You can't even believe it. He works for one of those brokerage places and thought he was such hot stuff, but the boy didn't even know how to order a decent red wine." She blew air between her lips. "Done with him. He hardly paid attention to me because he was watching everyone else in the restaurant, hoping that he might see someone that he knew."

That would have been hell for Bunny. You either paid attention to her or she threw a tantrum so you couldn't help it.

"I'll bet that was awful," Polly said. "Why were you out with him?"

"Oh, Debbie Burns set us up. Somebody her boyfriend knew. You remember Debbie, don't you?"

Polly had no idea who Debbie Burns was, but this conversation could go on forever if she didn't bring a halt to it. "Why don't we meet at The Paramount at eleven? Will that give you enough time?"

"I'm so excited. I can't wait to see you, Polly. I have so many things I need to tell you."

"Awesome. I'll see you there." That would give Polly plenty of time to find something decent to wear and at least put some makeup on. She hadn't been to a hair stylist yet. That needed to happen this next week. She shook her head. There were so many things that needed to happen.

Steve Cook and Polly had spoken several times in the last two weeks. He was working with a realtor that was the son of one of Everett's friends. Rory Chandler and Polly had dated once in high school, but at the end of the evening, neither were interested in pursuing a relationship. Dating in high school was so much easier than doing so later in life, even though it didn't feel like it at the time. Because you went to class with the person every day, you just had to deal with it and move on. She and Rory saw each other several times throughout the years, the last time at her dad's funeral.

Rory and Steve were looking for the perfect location for Polly, but hadn't found anything yet. She was certain that something would turn up soon. It had to. She was moving back to Iowa in April whether a plan was in place or not.

Just the thought of that made her stomach leap. Polly wasn't sure if it was excitement, terror, or maybe a bit of both. Never before had she moved forward without a plan fully set in place, but that little piece of her gut that had kept her away from Joey's advances told her this was the perfect move.

Right now, a moving container was scheduled for just after the first of April. They'd store it in Iowa until she had a location. The next thing she needed to do was rent an apartment in Ames – something furnished and short-term. This was going to come together. Polly just knew it.

~~~

The hostess offered to seat Polly several times, but rather than tie up a table waiting for the perennially late Bunny, Polly chose to wait at the front. She checked the time on her phone once more. Bunny was now twenty-five minutes late. Five more and Polly was leaving. She'd sent two texts, neither of which had been answered. That wasn't new for Bunny. When she got caught up in something, she ignored everything else.

"*Five minutes and I'm out of here,*" Polly texted.

"*Coming around the corner now. Ta!*" Bunny responded.

Sure enough, there was no acknowledgment or apology. The front door opened and Bunny blew in. Dressed in heels that would send Polly into agonizing pain after five minutes, navy leather pants, and a bright blue belted jacket, Bunny looked fabulous. She always looked fabulous. Not comfortable-in-her-skin fabulous like Sal, but grabbing-all-the-attention fabulous.

"What do you think?" she asked, twirling around. "I picked this up after work yesterday and couldn't wait to wear it."

"You look amazing," Polly said. "You always look amazing."

"I do, don't I?" Bunny kissed Polly on both cheeks. "You've lost weight. We should find you some new clothes today."

Polly just smiled and nodded at the hostess.

"This is your party?" the hostess asked.

"Today *is* going to be a party," Bunny replied. "Let's get started. How about something to drink? Champagne?"

Polly shook her head. "Not if you're dragging me into shops this afternoon. No, I'm having a cappuccino and so are you."

"That's no fun." Bunny stuck her lower lip out. "I thought we were going to have fun today."

"So two cappuccinos?" the hostess asked after they'd been seated.

When Polly nodded, she went on. "I'll send your waitress right over."

"This is going to be awesome. We never go shopping anymore," Bunny said. "I saw the cutest bag over at Hermes. I think you should get it."

"Probably not," Polly said. "But we can go look."

"I need some new shoes. Mother says that her friend Judy has a nephew who will be in town this week looking for a job. He's coming up from Savannah and I'm going to escort him around town. Doesn't that sound like fun?"

"I guess. Uhh, Bunny, I need to tell you something."

"Can it wait?" Bunny brought her bag up and took out a small, wrapped package. "I bought this for you when I was up in Rockport last weekend with Mother and Daddy."

Polly took the package. "Should I open it now?"

"Of course, silly." Bunny waved her fingers. "Go on. Hurry."

Carefully peeling back the tape, Polly unwrapped the package of salt water taffy. "You know me so well."

"I bought an assortment, but added extra peanut butter and caffe latte in there because I *do* know you."

"Thank you, Bunny. This is really sweet."

They stopped talking as the waitress brought their drinks and menus. "I'll be back in a moment to take your order."

Bunny nodded and then asked, "Can we still get breakfast?"

"You sure can," the young woman responded.

"Good," Bunny said to Polly. "I don't want anything heavy like a sandwich and I'm tired of eating salads. I've been eating those all week long." She ran her hand down her side. "But I fit into these pants this morning, so it was worth it, don't you think?"

Polly laughed. "I said it before. You look amazing."

"You have to say that. You're my friend." Bunny put her menu down on the table. "I'll just have the oatmeal."

"Are you kidding me?" Polly asked. "You're about to walk three hundred miles this afternoon. Eat a real breakfast."

"You don't have to work to keep your weight down like I do," Bunny responded. "I don't know what you did to lose all of this weight, but I think I hate you for it. No matter what I do, I can't eat anything fun or it goes straight to my thighs. Mother says I have my grandmother's hips. Not her mother, but Daddy's. If I'm not careful I'll blow up like an upside-down balloon."

'Your mother said that to you?" Polly shook her head.

"She's just trying to help me. She wants me to find a really terrific man so that I can be happy like she's happy with Daddy."

"Has it never occurred to you that you can be happy without a man?"

"Bite your tongue, Polly Giller. Not all of us are as confident as you. And besides, I like it when men pay attention to me."

"I didn't say that I don't like it, but I just think that when you're comfortable with yourself first, a relationship with your boyfriend or husband will be that much better."

"Speaking of relationships, how are things with Joey?"

"We broke up. And that's one of the things I wanted to talk …"

Bunny interrupted her. "You broke up? Did you break up with him or did he break up with you? He was kind of a catch. So good looking and he has all that family money and he had the hots for you." She glared at Polly. "You broke up with him, didn't you?"

"Yeah. I did. But that's not all there is to the story."

"It doesn't really matter. You just don't get it. Men like that don't grow on trees. He would do anything for you."

Polly put her hand up to get Bunny's attention. "Stop just a minute. Joey was an obsessive creep. He started beating other men up just for talking to me."

"What? That's crazy. I can't believe it. He was raised better than that, wasn't he? Come on, you've got to be messing with me."

"No, Bunny. He went to jail for beating the hell out of a guy in a club simply because the guy caught me when I tripped."

"Why didn't you tell me this before? Did you think I wouldn't understand? My goodness, Polly. You get yourself in the craziest situations. How come I didn't know?"

"Because I was trying to keep it quiet just in case things worked out with me and him," Polly said. "But I want to tell you something else."

"You thought things were going to work out with him after he got out of jail? How much longer did you two date? Was he changed by being in jail? What did his parents say about that? You never tell me anything." Bunny sat back in her chair and crossed her arms. "Sometimes it is so hard to be your friend. I feel like you hold me at arm's length, only letting me in every once in a while. How long have you been broken up with him?"

"I don't know. That's really not my big news, Bunny." Polly sighed when the waitress approached their table again.

"Are you ready to order?"

Polly pointed at the menu. "I'll have the Reuben and fries." She tapped her mug. "And another one of these."

They both looked expectantly at Bunny, who was flipping her menu back and forth.

"I thought I just wanted oatmeal, but Polly says I should have something more since we're going to be shopping this afternoon. I don't know what I want, though." Bunny ran her finger up and down the menu, flipped it over to the other side and did the same again. "Fine. I'll have the Asian chicken salad. But I want the dressing on the side. Can you put the chow mein noodles and the chicken on the side too? I don't know if I want to eat all of that."

The waitress nodded and took the menus back. "Would you like another coffee?"

"No, bring me sparkling water, please," Bunny said, then turned back to Polly. "Now what were you saying?"

Polly waited until the waitress left. "I'm moving back to Iowa."

Bunny had opened her mouth to say something else and promptly closed it. She stared at Polly in shock.

"No words?" Polly asked.

"You're what?"

"I'm moving back to Iowa. I quit my job and hired a moving company. After I sell my car and pack my things, I'm flying back in April."

"You can't leave me," Bunny said. "What will I do without you? Why would you do this to me?"

"Because I need to change some things in my life."

"But what about me? I'm not ready to have you leave town. I'll never get to see you again." She flung her napkin on the table. "This is awful. Why are you waiting until now to tell me? I suppose you told your friend, Sal, already."

"Actually, no," Polly said. "I haven't. I'm sorry to spring it on you, but Bunny, this whole thing with Joey showed me that I'm not really living much of a life here. I only have a few friends and my job. Don't you think a person needs more than that?"

"You just need to find the right man. Then you'd settle down and get to know more people. You could get to know his friends and their wives. That would be a whole big new set of friends for you. Tell me you won't leave until I think about who to introduce you to. I'll even ask Mother to help. She likes you well enough and she knows tons of eligible young men. For heaven's sake, she's been trying to find the perfect one for me. Maybe one of those would work for you."

Polly reached across the table and took Bunny's hand, effectively silencing her. "Stop. I've already made the decision. My accountant is looking for a place in central Iowa for me to renovate. I want to dig into something and find a life that's bigger than just ..." she paused. "Bigger than this. I know it doesn't make sense to you. It may never make sense. But it's what I need and I want you to be happy for me."

Bunny's lower lip went back out. "But I *don't* understand and I'm not happy at all. Not at all. You can't move away. You just can't." She crossed her arms again. "And now I don't even feel like shopping. You've ruined the whole day. Waitress?" Bunny waved her arms. "Waitress!"

Their waitress came back to the table. "Yes?"

"Bring me an order of those sweet potato fries, too. I need comfort food. I just received the worst news ever. My best friend is moving and she waited until today to tell me. Make it a double order. We'll share."

The girl nodded. "I'll get those right in."

"Honey, you have to figure out how to be okay with this," Polly said after the waitress walked away. "I don't want you to be mad at me. This isn't about you. I need something more in my life."

"Your friends should be enough," Bunny said. "I'm going to miss you."

"I'm going to miss you, too. But when I get settled, you can come out and see what crazy things I've gotten up to. Promise?"

Bunny huffed. "I don't know. Flying clear out to Iowa seems like it would take forever. Do jets even go there?"

"Of course they do," Polly said with an uncomfortable laugh. "Iowa is as up-to-date as anyplace else in the country. They even have electricity and running water."

"Oh stop it," Bunny said. She giggled. "I deserved that. Polly, what am I going to do without you? Nobody lets me go on like you do. You always understand me and tell me that I'm amazing - even when I'm not. I don't know how I'm going to get through my life with you all those states away."

"You'll be just fine," Polly said. "And you can call me any time you want. We'll talk for hours."

"We better." Bunny took a long breath and let it out slowly. "I'm going to miss you."

CHAPTER NINE

Early March

"Stupid boxes," Polly said as bundles of them fell out of her arms. She finally got the key into her front door and pushed it open. As she bent over, her phone rang. "Just a minute," she muttered. "I'll get to you as soon as I can."

Kicking the boxes inside, she dropped the bag of tape and markers on the side table and reached into her back pocket.

"Hey, Steve, what's up?"

"We found it," he said.

"What? You found it? What did you find?"

"This great old school building in Bellingwood. You know where that is, right?"

It had been fifteen years since Polly lived in Iowa. "Not really. Cool name for a town, though. Where is it?"

"Just west of Ames and a little north of Boone. Does that help?"

Polly put him on speaker and opened the map application on her phone, then searched for Bellingwood. "Oh. I see. How many people live there?"

"About fifteen hundred, but the area is growing."

"And the school is for sale?"

"Yeah, and you can't believe the price. It's been vacant since the late nineties and they are desperate to get rid of it. Rory says that if they can't find a buyer in the next year, they're taking the building to the ground and will re-zone the land."

She sat down on the edge of her sofa and expanded the map, then flipped over to the satellite view. Sure enough – a big old schoolhouse. A creek ran along the back side of the land and there was a concrete pad just to the south of the building. It was in a prime location, just off the highway. "It's a schoolhouse," she said.

"You don't sound very excited. It's exactly what you asked for. Two stories, immense rooms upstairs. There's an auditorium, room for classrooms downstairs and maybe an office. The old kitchen is there. You'd have to get new appliances and re-wire things, but it's a steal.

"Looks like some of the windows are broken out. Is the mess inside really awful?"

"I haven't seen it yet; just got the news this morning. Rory was looking closer to Story City and east of the interstate. Then out of the blue, he came across this. Do you want us to pursue it?"

"Send me the link for the sale site," Polly said. "I want to look at it more closely."

Steve hesitated. "You don't sound as excited as I thought you would. Isn't this what you were looking for?"

"Yeah. I suppose. But now that it's real, I want to be absolutely sure." Polly chuckled. "To be honest, I thought I'd have longer to plan. I figured I'd be living in Ames for at least a year before I needed to make any kind of decision."

The cost of living in Iowa was much less than Massachusetts. Her savings would allow her to live without any extra income for several years. She'd been looking forward to the idea of traveling around the state while searching for the perfect place to settle.

"What do you want me to do?"

"Send me the link and give me a day to think about this. Do you think I should fly back to Iowa to look at it?"

"You'll be here in less than a month, right?"

"Yeah. But if it's the right place for me, do I need to worry about losing it?"

"Nobody has looked at this place in years. They just dropped the price again so that might bring out a few more interested parties, but I doubt it. You take a look and call me in a couple of days. I'll tell Rory to keep an eye on it for us. If something else comes up, we'll stay in touch."

"Thanks, Steve. I'll talk to you later."

Polly sat back and looked at the satellite imagery of Bellingwood. It looked like a regular Iowa small town. One street for the downtown area, some manufacturing to the south of the old school, little homes everywhere and farmland surrounding it as far as the eye could see. Being close to Boone and Ames was nice. She did a few calculations in her head. It was about forty-five minutes north of Des Moines, so she could at least get there and back from the airport in short order.

"What do you have for me, little town in the middle of Iowa?" she asked, tapping the phone.

Her phone dinged with Steve's incoming email and Polly picked up the laptop from the coffee table. She wanted to spend time with this.

~~~

Pounding at her front door brought Polly out of a drowsy sleep. She jumped to her feet and stumbled over the stacks of boxes she'd left where they landed.

"Who's there?"

"It's Sal. Bunny Farnam just called me. You're moving?"

That little bitch. Polly didn't know whether to be furious or terrified at the prospect of having to tell Sal after she heard about this from someone else. Her heart raced as she put her hand on the door knob.

"I'm sorry, Sal," Polly said as her friend pushed past her into the front room.

"What is this? You're really moving? I told her that she was crazy. You wouldn't make a decision like that without talking to me, but apparently you have." Sal turned on Polly, betrayal written all over her face.

"I was going to tell you. It's just that everything happened and then …" Polly closed her mouth. "I have no excuses. I'm sorry."

"Why are you moving? Where are you going?"

"Back to Iowa. I can't stay here any longer."

"What does Iowa have that Boston doesn't?" Sal put up her hand. "Don't even try to answer that. They have nothing on us. You will never find all the museums and the history we have here. Hell, I bet you can't even find good coffee shops out there. And *I'm* here. Doesn't that count for something? How long have you been planning this?" She shook her head. "I suppose this is all my fault. I knew you were having trouble after Joey screwed up so bad and I've been so busy that I didn't take care of you. I'm really sorry about that, Polly, but please don't move."

"No, no, no. It's nothing about you." Polly took Sal's arm and led her over to the sofa. "It's all about me. And it's my fault for not telling you sooner. I knew you were busy and I didn't know how I was going to tell you. I guess I just figured that at some point it would come up and then it would be over. I'm really sorry."

"Well, it's come up."

Polly glared at Sal. "Why did Bunny call you? Just to tell you about me leaving Boston?"

"Yeah." Sal nodded. "She seems to think you're out to destroy her life."

"Of course I am. But you two barely know each other. What was she thinking?"

"Well, she asked if I could stop you from making this terrible mistake." Sal looked around at the boxes. "It's a little late for that, though, isn't it?"

"I quit my job two weeks ago," Polly said.

"And you didn't think this was information I needed to have?"

'I know. I feel terrible. I really wanted to take you out to lunch and tell you everything. You should have heard it from me first."

"Yes. I should have heard it from you. I thought we were better friends than this."

"We are." Polly shook her head. "It's just that Bunny called me on Saturday to go shopping and I figured it would be the last time I ever saw her, so I wanted to get it over with. It never occurred to me that she would call you and tattle."

"Is this because of what happened with Joey?" Sal asked.

"That was the trigger." Polly pointed at a stack of hand-written letters. "He's not letting this go and I don't want to fight with him."

"So you're just running away. That's not the Polly Giller I know. I'm ashamed of you."

Polly grinned. "Shame won't work, Sal. I said he was the trigger, but he isn't the whole story." She stood and paced over to the television and picked up a framed photograph of her and her father sitting in one of his tractors. "You know I don't have much of a life here. I don't run in any social circles. I worked, spent time with you or Drea or Bunny … or Joey, and then came home. All of our other friends from college have moved on. We haven't seen those girls in a couple of years."

"I have," Sal said quietly. "You just got busy with Joey and quit coming to the parties."

"The parties were boring. You said so yourself. There's only so much I can take of those girls." Polly crossed her arms. "I thought you said you were done with them."

"We have lunch every once in a while. It's interesting to hear what they're doing. You should come." Sal pushed a half empty box that was sitting on the floor in front of her. "Oh. That's right. You're leaving town."

"Don't be that way. Tell me you get it about my life," Polly pleaded.

"I really don't." Sal crossed her long legs in front of her and sat back. "You could decide to get involved in something. Volunteer. Join a church. Join a club. I don't know. What do WASPie girls like you do to make friends?"

"That's it, exactly," Polly said. She strode across the room and sat back down beside Sal. "I have no idea. I've lived here for fourteen years and haven't figured it out yet. I've dated men that don't hold my interest and the one who finally did turned out to be a psycho stalker. I'm failing at this life and it's time for me to do something different. The one place on earth where I know that could happen is in Iowa."

"You're moving home?"

"Not home. I don't want to move home. I don't want to be Everett Giller's daughter who gave up on her life in the big city. I want to move somewhere and make my own name. Be my own person. Do something fantastic." Polly opened the laptop again and clicked through to the link Steve had sent her. "Look at this."

"I see an old dump of a building."

"Exactly. I can afford to buy this and renovate it. It's stupid cheap right now. With the money I've saved, I can also afford to live in a furnished apartment in Ames as long as necessary. Iowa's cost of living is nothing like what we know here."

"You live like a monk already," Sal said. "That's probably why you haven't met people. You're so darned frugal. Look at this place. You barely decorated it."

"I know. It's like I knew this wasn't my home - I was just existing in the space. I want to go somewhere and turn it into my home."

"I still can't believe you haven't involved me in any of these things you were thinking about. Are you going to buy that building?"

"It's an old school and I don't know yet. Steve just called me about it today. I've been staring at these pictures all morning trying to decide if this is where I want to start my new life."

"Bellingwood. That's a weird name."

"But it's kinda cool, don't you think?"

Sal took a breath and slumped her shoulders. "You're really doing this?"

Polly shook her head. "I don't know. Honestly, I thought it would take more time to find something. There's no reason for me to hurry. Who knows - the town might suck. My luck it's a bedroom community and everybody works in Boone or Ames. If they're always leaving town, it will be hard to make friends."

Sal pointed at the picture of the school. "What do you want to do with a building that big?"

"This side on the main level is the old auditorium." Polly clicked through to a picture. "That's a stage there. Wouldn't it be fun to have bands come in and host dances and parties? And look at this big room over here. What if I put a little shop in there? I could sell used books and maybe bring ladies in to teach crafts. You know – knitting, crocheting, and maybe sewing. Then I could learn how to do those things, too."

"Did you suddenly become ninety-three?"

Polly pursed her lips. "Stop it. Think about how relaxing it would be. I could meet a ton of people if I just had a place for women our age to hang out when they needed a break from their families." She clicked to another space. "We could even have a daycare for their kids in the auditorium. Make it a place for kids to play and moms to relax. How cool would that be?"

"Not cool. It's weird. Are you planning to pay someone to watch all of those dirty snot-nosed rug rats?"

"Well, yeah. I don't have any details worked out. Until I saw the pictures, I had no idea."

"These pictures are empty shells of rooms. How do you see anything in them? Look at the broken windows and crap on the floors. The walls are destroyed."

"But you have to look beyond that. Dad always talked about houses that had good bones. If the structure is solid, everything else can be renovated - new walls, new carpet in the auditorium. Think about big, beautiful stage curtains in that room." Polly swiped to another photograph. "And look at this immense kitchen. Can you imagine how much fun it would be to cook in there with all that space? A great big prep table in the middle with deep sinks and one of those industrial stoves? How fun."

"Yeah," Sal said, her voice flat. "So much fun. Do they have takeout in town?"

"I'm sure there are restaurants. When I was looking at the map of the town, I saw a pizza place."

"At least there's that. No coffee shop?"

Polly shook her head. "But maybe I could put one in that kitchen. Let people know that it's there. I could make light breakfast stuff and coffee."

"There's no way you can make a business out of this."

"Why not?"

"There aren't enough people in the whole state to make it worthwhile."

Polly scooted away from Sal. "I think I can. I don't know for sure what I'll do, but there's no reason not to try. You have to get behind me on this. You just have to."

"I don't want to."

"Because I didn't tell you first?"

"You don't get it, do you," Sal said, frowning at Polly. "I don't want you to go back to Iowa. You'll get stuck there and I'll never see you again. You'll meet some farm boy, get married and have passels of children. When will you ever be able to travel back to Boston to see me?"

"You'll have to come to Iowa to see me."

"No. Freakin'. Way," Sal said. "I'm not coming out there. I'm probably allergic to corn stalks and you can't tell me that there are enough good men in a little town in the middle of Iowa to make it worth my time and effort."

"But I'd be there with my passel of babies." Polly burst out with a stilted laugh. "I don't even want babies. What am I saying?"

"That you should change your mind and stay in Boston. Make your best friend a happy, happy girl."

"What if this makes *me* a happy, happy girl?" Polly asked.

Sal huffed. "Fine. But I'm still not going to like it. When do we start packing your stuff?"

"Right now?"

CHAPTER TEN

Mid-March

"I'd like a real, paper map. Do you have any here?" Polly asked the young man at the rental car counter.

He tilted his head and with a small smile, said, "You know the car has turn-by-turn GPS. It will take you wherever you want to go."

"I'd rather have a map," she said. "Those GPS-things make me nuts. Besides, I want to know more than just where I'm going."

"There's one here somewhere. Nobody wants maps anymore." He turned and called to the back. "Do you have any of those maps back there?"

Another young man in a blue vest walked out with a stack of paper maps. "Here. Do you need more than one?"

Polly chuckled. "One should do it. Thanks."

She'd gotten more and more excited about the idea of purchasing the school building, so she left her apartment in a complete mess and flew to Iowa to see if this really was a good idea. She was meeting Steve Cook at a restaurant in Ames for lunch before heading to Bellingwood. It was hard to believe this dream might come true.

Once she got on the interstate, she took in a deep breath and smiled. The sky was clear and the sun shone down, warming the cool March air. It felt like a lifetime had passed since the last time she drove this route. Des Moines continued to transform and change. She supposed that Boston did, too. If she left there for several years, things would become less familiar. Polly could hardly wait for this trip to become old hat - to know the street names and skyline so well that nothing surprised her.

After a short drive, she was out of the city and saw nothing but fields. "I'm home, Dad," she said, choking up. "You'd laugh at me for getting emotional, but I really missed this. Can you believe I took cornfields for granted?" Polly pointed at a small herd of cattle. "And cows. I took them for granted when I lived here. You don't see many cows in downtown Boston. Look at that, Dad. Open fields as far as I can see. Did you think I'd ever fall in love with this?"

Polly shook her head. When she was in high school, it never occurred to her that she would live anywhere but Iowa, though she was desperate to get out of Story City. Her original plan had been to go to Iowa State, but then, out of the blue, the scholarship had come through from Boston University and she never looked back. Everett put her on a plane that first year, promising to come out for parents' weekend. She'd been terrified, but excited at the same time. And then she met Sal - a force to be reckoned with. Even though Sal's family lived in the city, the girl refused to live at home. She wanted the entire experience of college and couldn't believe she was going to live with someone from Iowa. Polly was pretty sure Sal half expected her to wear bib overalls and carry bits of straw to clean her teeth. Polly might have been quite naive about a great many things, but the two girls had become fast friends.

She took the exit onto Highway 30 and drove west into Ames. This had changed quite a lot, too. A turn north onto Duff and Polly kept an eye out for Hickory Park. Steve asked if she liked barbecue. Well, of course. Who didn't? The truth was, though, she wasn't hungry. The idea of waiting to see the school building and the little community of Bellingwood was killing her.

Once in the parking lot, Polly looked around to see if Steve was waiting. She parked and took out her phone. *"I'm here. Are you inside?"*

"I see you. Sit still. I'm almost at your car."

Polly turned the car off and opened her door when she saw Steve approach.

He hugged her. "Are you ready for lunch?"

Looking at the front door, she sighed. "I suppose."

"What's wrong?"

"I don't feel like eating. I just want to see the place. I'm so excited I could pop."

Steve let out a laugh. "Just like your dad. Once he got something in his head, nothing could get in his way. Do you want to drive or do you want me to drive?"

"Are you in a hurry to be anywhere today? You could leave whenever you needed to if I just followed you there."

"I'm all yours. I figured you might want to spend time driving around the town."

"Then I'll drive, if you don't mind."

"Not at all." Steve walked around to the passenger side and waited for Polly to unlock the car door.

"Your car will be fine here?" she asked.

"No worries. Just head back out on the highway and I'll tell you when to go north."

Polly buckled in and drove back to the entrance. She waited for a small break and darted across four lanes of traffic, then headed for the exit.

Once she was on the ramp for the highway, Steve let out his breath. "Whoa."

She glanced at him and laughed out loud. "Did I do something wrong?"

"No, but that was just a little scary. Iowans don't drive like that."

"Oh," she said, still laughing. "I'll try to slow down some. But we'd still be sitting there if I hadn't jumped out into traffic."

"And my heart would still be beating at a normal rate." He patted her hand. "It's okay. I'm working to bring it back into regular sinus rhythm. Speed limit is sixty-five here, though. Just saying."

"Got it."

"City folk," he muttered.

"Sorry."

"S'alright." He grinned at her. "Are you packing for the big move?"

"I sold my car this weekend. It's starting to become real. It feels a little weird, you know."

"What's that?"

"Moving back to Iowa. I didn't think I ever would, especially after Dad died. I figured I'd come back at some point to deal with all of his things in that storage unit, but that would be the last time."

Steve pointed. "Turn right here."

Polly followed his direction. "How far?"

"Less than ten miles. You're going to turn west at the big cellular tower."

"What?" she asked, laughing. "Maybe I should look for the blue house on the corner with a yellow dog in the driveway?"

"I think it's a white house," he replied, deadpan.

True to his word, a big cell tower loomed in the distance and Polly headed straight for it, slowed for the corner, and turned left.

"Just a few miles and you'll see the outskirts of Bellingwood," he said. "There's a steakhouse on the edge of town where we could eat when we're finished. Last week, I also found a diner downtown."

"Iowa diner?" Polly lit up. "Pork tenderloins and hot beef sandwiches?"

"I'm sure."

"That's where I want to eat if we have time. So, how's Jen?"

"She's good," he said. "Six years cancer free now. We're in

extra innings and loving it. With the kids out of the house, we do more traveling in the summer when Jen's not teaching. We're going to Georgia in June before it gets too hot. She's got a cousin in Savannah who invited us to stay with them."

"Do you still camp at the State Fair?"

"Every year. Beth and Nick have started bringing their campers. You know Beth has a baby now."

Polly let out a small laugh. "Everybody keeps growing up. How about Nick?"

"No kids yet. They're in no hurry." He pointed at a building on the right side. "That's the steakhouse. We're here."

She slowed and looked back and forth, trying to take it all in. The town was like every other small town she'd ever driven through, but somehow, Polly felt like she needed to absorb everything and make it hers.

"That looks bad," she said, pointing to an old run-down strip motel.

"The town has been through rough times just like every other small town in Iowa. Now slow down even more. You're going to see it up here on your left."

Polly thought her heart would leap out of her chest. No one was directly behind her, so she slowed to a stop at the corner. She wasn't sure what she expected, but there it was. The building had seen better days. Windows were broken out on the second floor and those on the first floor had been boarded up with plywood. The grass was brown and the parking lot was overgrown with weeds and dirt. What looked like a sidewalk was cracked and broken.

She turned into the parking lot. "Do you have keys to get inside?"

"I do," he said. "Rory couldn't be here today, but we have permission to go in. What do you think?"

"I thought I'd be more excited," Polly said, rolling to a stop in front of the main door. "This looks like a lot of work."

He nodded. "It will be, but isn't that what you wanted? To bring something like this back to life?"

Polly craned her neck as she turned to look behind them. "It looks like the whole town needs to be brought back to life."

"You just don't know the people yet," he said. "Once this place becomes home, you'll see it for the treasure it is."

"Why are you being so encouraging, Steve?"

"Come on. Let's go inside." He took out a flashlight. "The main level will be dark with all of the windows closed up."

Polly followed him to the front door. He fussed with the new lock that had been installed before opening the door. She stepped back at the overwhelming scent of mildew and rot.

"This place has been closed up for a long time," Steve said. "You have to use your imagination." He kicked a rock over to prop the door wide open and led her inside, then flipped on the flashlight.

"Seriously, why do you think I should be doing this?" Polly asked. "This is a huge endeavor."

Steve stopped in front of the stairs. She could still see his face in the light streaming in from the front door. He smiled. "Because, Polly, this is what you want. It's what you need. Your father would be thrilled to help bring something like this back to life. Do you have any idea what it will do for Bellingwood?"

She shook her head.

"A project like this injects life into a community. When people see things come back to life, it makes them want to do more of the same. Bellingwood is seeing hints of growth, but a big project like this would be fabulous for them. I talked to a buddy of mine whose uncle runs the general store downtown. I think he's part of the Chamber of Commerce. When I said something about finding an owner for this school, there was a lot of excitement. You come into Bellingwood with no preconceptions about the town. You don't know all of their petty fights and community issues. And the best thing you bring is Everett Giller's hopeful, positive attitude. That man knew how to rise above things and when it got rough, he just stuck right in there until it was better. He never gave up. You're his daughter, through and through."

"Wow," Polly said. "Thanks, but I'm not sure if you're right."

"I'm right. You're the perfect person for this project. The price is so good on this building, it would be a shame to let it get away. If we find the right contractor, this place will transform in a heartbeat. You just wait and see."

She nodded. "Okay. Let's look at it through my rose-colored glasses. It just overwhelmed me there for a minute."

"It's going to overwhelm you again and again, but you'll move past it. Let's go upstairs first."

They climbed the stairway to the second floor and Polly stood in the center of the immense hallway. "There's so much I could do with this," she said. "I could live over here." She turned to the right and walked into the first classroom. Leaves and trash covered the floor. "If we knocked out these internal walls, I could turn this whole side into an apartment."

Practically running, she darted back out and ducked into the other two rooms on that side, then dashed across to the other side.

"Steve?"

He caught up with her in the middle classroom. "What's up?"

"What was that concrete out there for?"

"That was the old gymnasium. It was dangerous, so they took it down, but the land would be all yours. You could do what you wanted with it."

Polly nodded and headed into the back classroom. She looked out over the yard filled with broken down playground equipment. "That all has to go. That creek is bank full. Is it always like that?"

"Spring thaws and lots of rain," he said. "I don't know if it's ever left its banks."

"Something to think about," Polly replied. She creased her forehead. "I don't know what those white trees are."

"Sycamore trees – they lose their bark in the winter. The creek is called Sycamore Creek since it's lined with them."

"Those are the great big huge leaves, aren't they? That'll be a terrible mess to clean up when they drop every fall." She stepped toward the doorway. "If I live on the other side, what would I do with these rooms?"

"Rent 'em out," Steve said.

She looked at him. "You think?"

He shrugged. "You could."

"Okay. That's interesting. Can I see what the downstairs looks like now?"

"It will be dark. What do you think so far?"

"I think that if you say I can afford this, I'd be crazy not to."

He led her back down the steps, turned his flashlight on and they carefully picked their way across debris toward the back of the building. "This is the old kitchen. The appliances were taken out, so it's just a shell." He ran his hand across the old serving counter. "This is still in good shape."

Polly nodded and pulled on a door. "This is the auditorium?"

"I'm sorry you can't see more of it. This room is dark with the windows closed up. The pictures they took are pretty definitive."

They walked back out into the main hallway and he shone the light into the classrooms on the south side.

"What else would you like to see?" he asked.

"I guess nothing right now." Polly scratched her head. "My head is spinning. All I see right now is the mess and the huge amount of work ahead. I need to step back so I can consider the possibilities."

"Are you so overwhelmed that you might walk away from it?" They went out and Steve kicked the rock away from the door and held it open. "Are you ready to leave?"

"Let's see what Bellingwood looks like. I want to eat at the diner. Maybe that will help me get a feel for the town."

"You didn't answer my question," he said, slamming the front door of the building shut before re-locking it. He tugged on the handle and walked with Polly to the car.

She went around to the driver's side and got in. When he was seated, she took a breath. "I don't want to walk away from it, but renovation will be impossible if I don't find just the right person to work with. I can't do this by myself."

"Then that will be the next thing we work on. Do you want me to pursue the purchase?"

Polly smiled as she pulled out of the parking lot onto the highway. "I think I do." She gave her head a quick shake. "I can *not* believe that I'm doing this. I wish Dad were here. It would be so much easier."

"If he were here, he'd be the one doing the work, not you," Steve said. "This is your dream. You can create anything you want."

"Now I just need to figure out what that looks like."

CHAPTER ELEVEN

First week of April

"Slow down," Drea snapped. "Be careful with that."

Her brother, Jon, just smiled and tipped the dresser back. "Hush, lil sis. We got this."

Ray Renaldi picked the bottom of the dresser up and the two carried it outside.

"I can't believe you're here today," Polly whispered. "I was going to just hire this done."

Drea shook her head. "When Mama found out that you were going to pay someone else to pack up your things she came unglued. She already threw a conniption at the thought of you leaving Boston. You're one of her family and she's not ready to see you go."

"But I explained it the other night at dinner. She seemed okay."

Drea patted Polly's arm. "That was while you were in the house. I've fielded at least three calls per day asking if I can't find a way to keep you from moving. When I explain that you already purchased a building to renovate and that you want to live closer to where you grew up, she hears what I say and then asks once more if I can talk you into staying. If you hadn't explained to her what that Delancy character did to you, she'd be even more insistent. But she understands what it means to escape from a psychopath."

Polly looked at her friend in confusion. "Your mother?"

"Oh," Drea said, shaking her head. "No. Not Mama. But her sister was married to an abusive man. Zia Lisa lived with us for two years when I was a little girl. Every time her husband got drunk, he'd show up at the front door, screaming for her to come out. Papa'd open the door holding his shotgun and just stand there. The guy worked on the docks and one day he just never came home. Zia moved back into their house, married Uncle Claudio and that was that. I don't even remember what her first husband's name was. It was as if he simply never existed."

"You have the funniest stories," Polly said. "I can't imagine growing up in your family."

"It's filled with loud crazy people, that's for sure." Drea took Polly's arm. "I'm going to miss you, Polly Giller. These last few years have been so special for me."

Polly pulled her into a hug. "I can't believe your whole family took me in. Your mother's house was always another home for me."

"It always will be. Mama would insist on that."

"Okay, what's this?" Sal asked, coming into the room. "Here I am working my fingers to the bone and the two of you are in here crying like a couple of schoolgirls."

Drea and Polly separated and Polly laughed. "To the bone?"

"Well, I'm telling those boys what to do. They'd have this place emptied in less than an hour if I wasn't out there slowing them down." Sal winked. "I'm not ready for you to go yet."

Polly smiled. "Before you know it, I'll invite you to come see my grand new home. There will be parties and dances, exciting events and wonderful people for you to meet."

"Maybe you'll finally find your personal dreamboat," Sal said. "And if you do, can you look for one for me, too?"

"How about you, Drea?" Polly asked her friend. "Shall I look for a man for you?"

"I'm perfectly happy with my life just the way it is," Drea said. She walked across the room and patted Sal's shoulder. "Though I'd pay good money to see what Sal Kahane would do to a nice boy from the Midwest."

Sal grinned. "Me too. That sounds like fun."

"Stop it. I grew up in Iowa and it's going to be my home again. I love those people," Polly said.

"Of course you do, sweetie," Sal replied. "We'll be good. I came in because the boys have nearly everything packed into the container. If you're finished here, the drivers are ready to take off."

Polly took a deep breath and paced the perimeter of her bedroom. "It's just a shell. All of those years and this room no longer feels like it's mine."

She'd been through the cupboards over and over, checking to make sure nothing was left, then cleaned each room as she emptied it. The kitchen cupboards and appliances were cleaner than they had been when she moved in. Her landlord had walked through last night and told her to just lock her keys inside. They'd take it from there.

"Are you okay?" Sal asked.

"I'm going to miss you so much, but I'm excited. Like crazy excited," Polly said. "I'm meeting with a couple of contractors this week. I hope one of them will be perfect for the job."

"I hope he's cute and single."

Polly swatted at her. "Stop it. I'm not moving to Iowa to find a man to marry. I'd be perfectly happy to be Polly Giller for the rest of my life if I could just do something that's worthwhile."

"I know, I know," Sal said. "You can't stop a girl from hoping, though, can you?"

"Of all the people I know," Polly said, "you are the last one I would expect to harass me about finding a man."

Sal dropped her head. "I'm so ashamed."

Polly laughed. "No you're not. Stop it."

"I am a little bit. Whatever makes you happy. You know that's what I want for you, right? And the fact that you're putting twelve hundred miles between you and that jerk who scared you to death makes me very happy. Speaking of which, have you heard from him lately?"

"I don't know," Polly said with a shrug. "I forwarded my mail to a post office box in Bellingwood. There will probably be a bunch of mail there when I arrive, but at least I haven't had to look at it for the last few days." She shrugged. "But I actually hadn't seen anything from him for over a week. He was letting up. Maybe the fact that I ignored him finally got through that thick skull."

She stood in the middle of the living room and looked around. This wasn't her home any longer. It didn't even look familiar.

"Are you ready to shut this door?" Sal asked.

"Yeah," Polly said with a small nod. "I think I am. Let's do this."

The two went outside after she pulled the door shut. Drea and her brothers were talking to the two young men from the moving company.

One looked up and saw Polly, then approached with a clipboard. "We're ready to take off, Miss Giller. It looks like we're just parking the container at the lot in Ames until you're ready for it. That right?"

"Yeah. That's right."

"Then sign here and here." He pointed at the paperwork. "Here's your claim card and location number. You can check with the yard on Thursday. It should be in place and waiting for your next move. Any questions?"

Polly looked at Ray. "Everything packed in there?"

"Snug as a bug in a rug," he said.

"Then no questions. Thanks, guys."

"See you on the other side."

She gulped as the truck drove off. "I can't believe that just happened. This all got real."

Jon laughed. "More real than the day you signed paperwork to buy that monstrosity in central Iowa? I would have thought that was real."

"Okay. That was pretty real, but this means I have to do something about it all now. I could have owned that building for years and just lived here around all of you."

Sal grabbed Polly's hand. "Then do that. I'll run after the movers and tell them that you're not going anywhere. Stay. Stay."

They watched the moving truck turn a corner.

"I think I have to go," Polly said. "My things are heading to Iowa. I should probably follow."

"If we don't take you to the airport, you can't follow," Ray said. He picked Polly up and hugged her tight. "I'm going to miss you, little Miss Giller. You've been a bright spot in this city of dullards."

Polly laughed. "You're such a poet. And a crazy man."

"You marry her," Sal said. "Make her stay. Please?"

Jon Renaldi took Polly's hand and went down on one knee. "Polly Giller, will you marry me and stay in Boston?"

"Yes, Jon. I will," Polly said. She turned to wink at Drea. "On one condition."

"What's that?"

"That you promise to take my last name."

He jumped to his feet. "Mama would kill me."

"I know," Polly said with a laugh. She hugged him. "And your sister would do the same if you tried to marry me. How many times has she warned you away?"

Jon pouted. "She never lets me have any fun. She has the nicest girlfriends and they're all off limits. You'd think she didn't trust her brothers."

"I don't," Drea said. "You're worthless. Sal, do you want to ride with us to the airport? I'll bring you back here to your car."

Sal shook her head. "I need to work this afternoon. I'd love to, but duty calls."

Polly turned to wrap her arms around the girl who'd been such a part of her life for the last fourteen years. "Oh Sal, it's really real. I can't believe I won't see you tomorrow."

"Like heck you won't," Sal said, tears filling her eyes. "We'll video chat all the time until I come out to visit. God girl, I'm going to miss you. Call me the minute you land so I know you're safe, and don't let any cows chase you down the road. Okay?"

Polly laughed, though tears streamed down her face. "I'll miss you. I love you."

"I know." Sal gave Polly a weak grin, pulled away and practically ran to her car.

"You're knocking 'em off like flies," Jon said. "Who's going to be crying next?"

Drea hit her brother in the arm. "You are, punk. Now hug Polly and say goodbye. Both of you. Tell her how much you love her so we can get on the road."

~~~

Polly sank into her bed at the Des Moines Holiday Inn. She was finally here. Steve Cook's wife, Jen, had to be in Des Moines tomorrow, so she was going to pick Polly up and take her back to Story City. The last time Polly had been in Iowa to sign the paperwork, she'd retrieved her father's truck from storage. Steve took care of getting it checked out at the garage and now it was waiting for Polly. She'd also signed a short-term lease on a furnished apartment in Ames. The next things on her agenda were finding a company to clear the trash out of the old schoolhouse and hiring a contractor to help her rebuild the place.

For the last month, she'd spent every waking moment dreaming about the possibilities in front of her. While she packed boxes, she imagined what her apartment could look like. With the internal walls knocked out, she'd have an immense living space. The front room would be the kitchen and dining room. Hopefully there wouldn't be too much trouble running water that far. A large living room would fill the rest of the open area. The back room would be her bedroom and the contractor would put a bathroom in one corner. The tall windows would bring sunshine streaming in every morning. She could hardly wait.

Polly hoped that she'd get a chance to see wildlife, especially at the back of the school by the creek. She'd have to get a riding lawn mower to deal with the huge yard. The city had kept the lawn cut back, but now that it was hers, they were finished.

Opening her phone, she quickly made a note to herself about getting a lawn mower. If not, she needed to find someone to take care of the mowing and trimming. She wanted the place to look nice. People in town would watch her every move, she was sure of that. When she lived in Story City, the fact that everyone knew what everybody else was doing seemed so natural. There were very few secrets in a small town. When Polly went home for holidays, she'd curl up on the sofa in the living room and listen as Mary and her father told her about the exciting and mundane things that happened to people she'd grown up with. The thing was, she barely remembered those stories now.

What kind of stories would she uncover in Bellingwood? The last time she'd driven through the downtown, Polly tried to take in all the small stores she saw, wondering who the owners were and how she might end up knowing them. When she drove past the elementary school, kids were everywhere. She'd stopped when a crossing guard stepped into the middle of the street and children ran after each other until the woman slowed them down. Busses waited in line for the kids who poured out of the building.

That day she'd driven all over the little town. Nothing was familiar and she was certain that it would take months or maybe even years for her to get to know people well. But that was okay. She had plenty of time.

Polly had no idea how long it was going to take to make the school building habitable. She feared it might take a couple of years, but hoped beyond hope that it wouldn't be that long. If she could be in her own apartment by Christmas, that would be a fantastic gift. Nothing would be more fun that decorating that big building with Christmas trees and white lights that would shine through those tall windows.

She couldn't believe her luck that the diner downtown had really good food. The pork tenderloin had been one of the best

Polly ever tasted. Their menu was made up of perfect Iowa diner food, but that tenderloin was what Polly would go back for. If she got tired of it, which seemed unimaginable, there were plenty of other things to try. She'd try the steakhouse out on the highway, too. When she was young, her father had a favorite steakhouse. Red crushed velvet wallpaper and dark wood were the things she remembered most. Well, that and the smoky interior. It was always dimly lit and Polly had vague memories of large groups of people sitting at big round tables.

Everything up to this point had focused on closing out her life in Boston. Tomorrow was the beginning of something new. Polly wasn't sure how she was supposed to go to sleep tonight.

CHAPTER TWELVE

"Hope we can work together," Stan Greaves put his hand out.
She shook it. "Thanks for your time."

As he walked away, she sat back down and drummed her fingers on the handle of her coffee mug. He hadn't understood what she was trying to do in Bellingwood. He said that he'd driven past the school and she'd sent sketches of her dreams for the building, but he insisted that a better plan would be for her to turn the entire place into condominiums because that was the big thing these days. He was the second contractor who assumed she was too young and too female to make good decisions. They had lots of advice to offer, but very little concern for her desires.

She had one more appointment with a small contractor who lived in Bellingwood. Steve Cook wasn't even sure how many big jobs the man had attempted. He was just re-starting his father's business and was hungry for work, so she hoped that would work in her favor.

Her phone rang and she smiled when she saw that it was Steve. After her interview with the first contractor yesterday, he'd been terribly apologetic. It made sense. Those men wouldn't speak to

Steve the same way they would a young woman, so he had no way of knowing what she had to face with them.

"Hey," she said.

"Was this one any better?"

"If you think turning the whole building into condominiums is better."

"No way."

"He hadn't even looked at the information I emailed to him."

"Oh Polly," Steve said. "I'm sorry."

"Not your problem," she said with a laugh. "I have to figure this out. You've done so much for me already, but I'm a big girl. If I end up with one of these men who wants to treat me like I don't know anything, I'll just pull up my jeans, strap on a sword and knock 'em around a bit."

"You'll what?"

She chuckled. "I had no idea where I was taking that analogy, so I just kept talking. But I can do whatever I need to do. I'd rather work *with* a contractor, but I can manage them if necessary."

"Your dad would be proud of you."

"I hope so. Now what's the name of this guy that I'm meeting again? Struthers?"

"Sturtz," Steve said. "Henry Sturtz. He seems like a nice enough guy. His dad was in the business for a long time. Retired a few years back and Henry's kept the company going, doing small jobs in the area. I did some checking on him. Seems like he does good work. He's got good references."

Polly nodded. While they talked, she pulled up the information Steve had sent her. "How old a man is he? If he's got his daddy's business, pretty young?"

"No," Steve said. "I'd say mid-thirties."

"Okay. So he's been around a while. The bio here says he went to Drake. That's kind of impressive for a contractor."

"Give me a call after you've met with him," Steve said. "I hope this one works out."

"Me too. I'm ready to get started. Thanks for everything, Steve."

"Talk to you later."

Polly picked her ticket up and went to the counter to pay. She was meeting this Sturtz guy at a coffee shop in Boone. It wasn't that far of a drive, but she hadn't been there in years and wanted extra time to familiarize herself with the town.

Once she got in her dad's truck ... her truck, she opened the glove compartment, hoping to find an old Iowa map. After she was finished with this appointment, she wanted to drive around the county. A pair of work gloves fell out onto the floor.

"What the ..." Polly leaned over and picked them up, then smiled. That's where her dad always stuck his gloves before coming into the house. He wanted to ensure they'd be there for him the next day. Polly brought the gloves up and smelled his cologne over the scent of the leather. "Oh Dad," she said. "I miss you. If you were here, I wouldn't have to learn all of this. I guess it's good for me, but I really do miss you." She tucked the gloves in her lap and drove out of the parking lot.

"Do you think this will be the guy for me?" she asked out loud. "I'm tired of being treated like a silly little girl." Polly chuckled. "That is not how you raised me. I might not know everything there is to know about construction, but that's not my job. Right?"

As she drove toward Boone, she sniffed the gloves once more and placed them on the passenger seat. "Did you know when you hired Steve that he was going to be so good for me? I don't know what I would have done these last couple of months. He made it easy for me to make good decisions. Thanks for that."

Polly passed a minivan filled with a young mom and three or four small children. The woman waved and smiled.

"At least she has children in the van to talk to. I'm just talking to a pair of gloves. Some people might think that was weird." She laughed again, suddenly feeling lighter.

Driving into Boone, Polly was thrust back into her childhood. Mary loved to drive through town with her, looking at the big old homes. They mused that the houses had been built during the height of the railroad. It was astonishing that they'd been kept in such great shape through all these years. Polly thought she'd like to see abstracts on those properties, just to uncover their history. Oh, the stories that might be hidden behind the walls of those homes - intrigue and murder, life and death. What was she thinking? The lives of the people living there were probably just as normal and boring as hers.

As she crossed Mamie Eisenhower Avenue, she remembered a trip she made with her dad. He wanted her to see the little house where the former first lady was born. Polly had been unimpressed at the time; the house was pretty small. But now that she was older it seemed more important. She'd need to make another trip.

Polly drove around the main shopping area of Boone, trying to commit to memory the various shops she might be interested in. She turned a corner and realized that she was in front of the coffee shop, so pulled into an open parking space.

Tucking the gloves back into the glove compartment, Polly took a deep breath. "This is going to be the one," she said. "I can feel it. Right, Dad?"

She tapped her steering wheel a couple of times, picked up the folder of sketches she'd made, and climbed down.

Once inside the coffee shop, Polly looked around. She was fifteen minutes early, so didn't expect he'd be here yet.

"Can I help you?" the young woman behind the counter asked.

"Just a cup of your dark roast," Polly said. She was going to be wide awake tonight after all the coffee and diet Mountain Dew she'd had today. It didn't help that the neighbors in the upstairs apartment were bent on partying their college career away. She remembered those days, so could hardly fault them, but their parents certainly wouldn't be happy when grades came out at the end of the semester. Polly had been lucky to room with Sal. Even though Sal was popular and loved to party, she'd had a good sense of when to stop and settle down.

She paid for her coffee and sat at a table near enough to the front door to be seen, but not so close as to be obvious. Each time the door opened, Polly's head shot up, but no one entered that might be a contractor. She opened her phone to check email and smiled at a message from Sal.

"I miss you! Have you found a contractor yet? I know you had some interviews today. I can't wait to hear all about your plans. Don't you dare do this without keeping me up to date. Bunny Farnam called again, whining about how you left town without saying goodbye to her. Seriously. Why isn't she calling you if she wants to complain? I don't need that crap. Mother set me up on another blind date with the nephew of one of her women's club ladies. This one might be the worst yet. He's an insurance salesman. Do you see me with someone like that? Oh come on, Mother. What are you thinking? Daddy just ignores it when I complain. Then he slips a hundred-dollar bill in my hand when I leave. I don't need his money, but I think it's his way of apologizing. Isn't it precious?"

"Miss Giller?"

Polly looked up to find an attractive, sandy-haired man standing in front of her. Dressed in jeans and a khaki work jacket, he had a genuine smile and intelligent eyes. She didn't know why those things occurred to her, but that's what she saw.

She stood up. "Yes. Are you Henry Sturtz?"

He nodded and pointed at her cup, then put his briefcase on an empty chair. "Do you want something to eat? They have great apple strudel here. I also really like their blueberry coffee cake."

"Twist my arm," Polly said. She walked toward the counter with him. "The coffee cake sounds good."

"I've got it. Go ahead. I'll be there in a minute."

She walked back to the table. So far, so good. She'd ended up paying for coffee for the last two contractors. This was definitely a step in the right direction. He wasn't bad to look at, either. "Stop it, Giller," she muttered. "Just stop it." She was glad that her back was to the counter so she didn't have to awkwardly watch him walk toward her.

He put his mug and two plates down. Moving the briefcase, he sat beside her rather than across the table. "This is one of my favorite places when I'm in town. Thanks for meeting me here."

"It's been years since I've been in Boone," Polly said. "But if I'm living in the area, it's time to get to know it better."

"You're staying in Ames right now?"

Polly nodded. "Until I get that old schoolhouse far enough along that I can move in. The drive isn't that bad."

"No, it's not. When I spoke with Mr. Cook, he said that you grew up in Iowa. That right?"

"Story City. Yes."

"And you went to college in Boston and stayed there? That had to have been a big change." He moved the plate with the coffee cake so it was directly in front of her. "And now you're coming back. It's going to be another big change."

"It already is," Polly said. "I'm a lot more relaxed. Things go so much slower around here." She rolled her eyes. "So. Much. Slower."

"Really?"

She laughed. "I nearly scared poor Steve … Mr. Cook … to death when I darted across traffic on Duff. He told me I could have waited. You never wait in Boston traffic. You move or you die. But people aren't in such a rush to do anything. Like here." Polly nodded at the counter. "She took my order and poured the coffee. Nothing was in a hurry. She didn't expect me to rush off to make room for the next customer behind me. When she took my money, it was almost slow motion, even though it's probably normal for you. Out east, she would have snatched the money out of my hand and had change back to me in seconds."

"Do you miss it?"

"Not at all. When I drove across on Highway 30 today, I didn't feel like I had to hurry; I could actually drive the speed limit. Most everyone else went around me, but nobody was upset about it."

Henry took a bite of his strudel. "You'll start going over the speed limit any day now. We aren't that slow around here. You'll catch up."

"But for now, I'm enjoying it," Polly said.

"Tell me what you're hoping for that old school building."

She smiled to herself. Nice start there, Henry Sturtz. "I have a lot of dreams for it. I want it to be my home, but I also want people in town to get involved. While I was sketching out some of the rooms, I thought about creating a place where we can hold classes - maybe craft classes or even computer classes. The kitchen is going to be one of the first rooms I want to renovate. Primarily for me to have a place to cook while I'm getting the rest of the place renovated, but I was thinking that it would be good to set it up for catering. The auditorium is a perfect place for events - maybe wedding receptions and office parties during the holidays. Someday down the road, I'd like to hire a chef to cater those events."

He nodded. "Your sketches show an apartment upstairs. That's where you want to live? And the rooms on the other side?"

"I know it sounds nuts," Polly said, "but I'd like to invite artists and authors to come to Bellingwood. It's so peaceful there. The school is on the edge of town. Only a couple of blocks to restaurants and shops, but with the creek behind the building and all that open space, it's the perfect place to let your mind rest and be creative."

"It doesn't sound nuts." He smiled at her. "It sounds nice. If you turned the two bathrooms into fancy spa baths, it would up the ante." Henry opened the briefcase, pulled out a set of blueprints and waited while Polly removed the napkin holder and other items from the center of the table. "I started putting ideas down on paper after you sent the email, and printed these out this morning. "If we knock out the stalls in the bathrooms, there is plenty of room to make them something special." He turned the page. "This was what I came up with for your apartment. I'd have to build a closet and bathroom back here for you, and this wall would pretty much stay in place. Well, except for the doors we'd cut out. Then, I was thinking we could build an entrance way for your front door. That would give you just a little bit of a hall for a coat rack or something."

"Wow," she said. "That's nice."

"There's an awful lot of wall space in that room. Do you have bookshelves that you'll be bringing in?"

Polly shook her head. "No, but I have books."

He laughed. "I assumed so since you're a librarian. It makes sense that you love books." He flipped another page. "I was thinking that I could install bookshelves along these walls and put up an entertainment center type thing as well. These old rooms need to have wood in them. They're so big, they need whatever we can give them to cut back on the echo."

"Okay, wow," Polly said. "You've given this a lot of thought."

"That old building has been a big part of Bellingwood. Most of us thought that it was just going to end up being razed to the ground. Getting the chance to restore it is kind of a thrill. It closed before I went to school there, but you'll meet a lot of people who have fond memories of their years in that building. You've got the whole town talking already, you know."

"I do?"

"Yeah. Everyone knows you bought it. They're just waiting to see what happens. Some say you're tearing it down to put up condominiums."

Polly laughed. "No."

"Yeah. And others think you're starting a commune or something."

"You're kidding."

"Kinda. But they'll be happy to see it come back to life. When the school closed, Bellingwood lost some of its heart. Losing it sucked the life out of the town. It will be interesting to see what you come up with."

CHAPTER THIRTEEN

Early July

Only two months had passed, but they had gotten so much finished. Polly sat in front of the old school building in Bellingwood, her stomach swirling in nervous anticipation. For the last two months, she'd spent every waking hour working here. They'd started by clearing out junk and debris from the interior. In the back of her mind, Polly had hoped they might uncover something fun left over from when the place was a school, but the building had been thoroughly emptied. There weren't even any blackboards left on walls in the classrooms. They'd cleared out more than a few bird's nests from the rooms upstairs and the exterminator had a long-term contract until the rodents and bugs were gone. Polly was tired of cleaning up mouse droppings. Somebody mentioned that she needed cats. She wasn't quite ready for that. Maybe someday.

Plywood was gone from the windows and glass replaced, making it much easier to see to work.

A few weeks ago, she cleared space in the basement. Today the movers would unload everything she'd brought from Boston. She wasn't ready to move into the building yet, but having access to her things again was an exciting thought.

She and Henry had put together a schedule of which rooms to complete first. The main kitchen was first on the list. If she had a kitchen and a working bathroom, she'd pitch a tent in the auditorium if necessary. Henry assured her that they would finish one room upstairs so she could move into the building within the next couple of months. Polly could hardly wait. Every day that she walked into the building, she could see progress.

The electricians were wiring the kitchen today. Henry recommended a local man named Jerry Allen, who had two young kids working for him as apprentices. Once they finished and the drywall was in, she'd paint the room and bring in appliances. Those had been a splurge, but Polly did her research first. After making calls to three clients of Steve Cook's who were restaurateurs, she'd landed on what she needed. Henry was building cabinets into one wall and she'd found a perfect eight-foot harvest table to place in front of the windows that looked out on the back yard. Right now, with the old playground equipment lying about, the yard wasn't attractive, but Polly had no trouble imagining it covered in lush green grass.

She was startled out of her reverie by a tap on the truck's door.

"Coming in to work today?" Henry asked.

"Just thinking about everything that was happening." Polly picked a box up from the passenger seat. "I stopped and got two dozen cinnamon rolls. Think that will make people happy?"

He took the box from her. "I think that will make people very happy. You're awfully nice to us."

Polly brandished a cup of coffee she'd picked up just as she drove out of Ames. "Will this make *you* happy?"

"Ah, Polly," Henry said with a laugh, stepping back so she could get out of the truck. "You know the way to a man's heart."

"If it's coffee, you're easy."

He muttered something as she unlocked the front door.

"What?"

"Nothing." He nodded for her to go on inside.

"No. I missed it. What did you say?"

Henry shook his head and laughed. "I just said that I really *am* that easy. But ignore me. It was a long weekend."

"Really?" Polly walked back toward the kitchen.

Even though it had yet to be finished, the room was still the gathering point for everyone who worked in the building. She'd purchased a large coffee pot and they ran an extension cord back here so there was always coffee available. The crews that were in and out of the building went through an ocean of coffee every day.

"What did you do this weekend?"

"My parents were here from Arizona and my sister came down from Michigan."

"That sounds like fun."

"It was. Mom and Dad are flying back out this week and Lonnie should be leaving in an hour or two to drive home."

"What were they here for? Anything special?" Polly went around behind the counter and picked up a tub filled with napkins, cups, coffee, sugar and creamer. She arranged things on the counter and took the coffee pot over to the utility sink to fill it.

"Dad's birthday. But Mom and Lonnie spent all day Saturday trekking through thrift stores for a new bedstead for Lonnie. They found what they wanted and now it's sitting in the shop so I can refinish it."

Polly chuckled. "That sounds like fun."

"Uh huh. I offered to build her a nice new bedstead, but she just couldn't help herself. The girl loves finding old junk to restore."

"Kinda like me and this place."

Henry pursed his lips. "So I have a type, huh?"

"What do you mean?"

"I end up working with people who like to restore things." He laughed. "You know. I would have been perfectly happy to build you a nice, new home somewhere in Bellingwood."

"And it wouldn't have been half as wonderful as this place is going to be when we're finished. Just think, this dirty old corner will come back to life."

"Yeah. It's going to be nice. People have been talking about how good it is to see cars in the parking lot again. You have to have a big open house so the town can come judge you on what you've done to the place."

"Judge me?"

Henry shook his head. "I shouldn't be like that. But you know, people talk and all. They're worried about an outsider moving into town and screwing up their ratty old school house." His eyes grew big as he laughed. "Makes me wonder if they are worried you're a Madame and might bring in ladies of the night."

Polly laughed until she snorted. "Oh, that's so me. But isn't it funny? I grew up in Story City. That's seriously just right down the road …"

"A piece?"

"What?"

"Right down the road a piece … get into the spirit of it, Polly."

She gave him a weak smile. "Okay. Weird. But anyway, I'm an Iowa girl just trying to get my life going again. It's not like I'm an outsider."

"You've been gone from Iowa for a long time."

"Surely they'll give me a break since I'm coming home."

He nodded. "It's not as bad as I make it sound. Ninety-eight-point-nine percent of Bellingwood is excited about what you're doing and look forward to seeing it happen. There are always sad sacks who will never be happy with what someone else does. The problem is, they make ninety-eight-point-nine percent of the noise."

"The reason they make all that noise is because no one listens," Polly said. She put coffee grounds into the filter and flipped the pot on. "I don't have time to worry about their noise, though."

"You're right. I shouldn't have said anything. I really just wanted to tell you that people are paying attention and for the most part, getting excited. Have you gotten any calls from the newspaper yet?"

Polly frowned. "Oh no. I'm not ready for that kind of attention."

"You're going to have it. This is a big deal. Can't you see it now? Local girl comes home from the big city. Film at eleven."

"Maybe I need to hire a media consultant," Polly said. "You know, to handle all the local gossip and the demands for my exciting life story."

"Who knows? Maybe your life is about to get really exciting."

She heard the front door open and in moments, two young men walked toward the kitchen.

"Hey boss," Jimmy Rio said. He looked at the spread on the counter. "Whoa. Is this for us?"

Polly pushed the stack of napkins toward him. "Help yourself. Coffee will be ready in just a few minutes."

The other young man, Sam Terhune, smiled. "Thank you. This is awesome."

"What's up, Jimmy?" Henry asked.

Jimmy turned, his mouth wrapped around a cinnamon roll, stumped as to whether to take the bite or remove the roll. He removed the roll. "We're working on the north side upstairs today, right?"

"Yeah. Hoffman's running pipe for the kitchen and bathroom first thing. If Ms. Giller's moving in, she should at least have a shower, don't you think? We need to finish knocking out the wall between the front room and middle room. Then measure for the bathroom door on the back wall. You can start framing the bathroom and closet in that back room, too."

"Got it."

The front door opened again.

"Hello? Is anyone here?"

Polly was already moving by the time two more young men came into sight of the kitchen.

"We've got a container of furniture to unload," the first said. His eyes caught the cinnamon rolls on the counter. A flicker of desire passed before he turned back to his buddy.

"That's for me," Polly said. "Would you like to join us?"

"What are you doing here?" he asked, glancing around. "Looks like a big project."

The other young man stepped up. "I heard about people buying old buildings and turning them into condos. That what you're doing?"

Polly shook her head. "No. Probably more of a community center kind of thing."

"Really? Is the city paying for it?"

She chuckled. "No. Not at all. It's a private business."

"Wow. Lots of money involved."

Henry stepped away from the counter, pulling Sam Terhune with him so they could make room for the newcomers. "Not all that much money when the owner is in here doing most of the work," he said, smiling at Polly.

"You're the owner?" the first mover asked Henry.

Henry shook his head. "Not me. I'm just her gopher."

The second turned to Polly. "You're doing all this by yourself? Who taught you to do construction?"

She really wasn't sure what to say. Henry had started something she had no idea how to undo.

Fortunately, he stepped forward. Clapping the first young man on the back, Henry said, "This is a learn-as-you-go project. We figure that the old building is in such bad shape we can't make it any worse. You two have enough help to bring Ms. Giller's stuff in and take it to the basement, right? Grab a cinnamon roll and we'll get started. What do you think, Polly? Bed upstairs in the middle room for now?" He handed the young man a napkin. "You wrapped the bed for her so it will stay clean, right?"

"Well ..."

"These aren't the two that packed my apartment," Polly said, coming to his rescue. "But yeah. We wrapped the mattresses. I didn't know how long they'd be in storage."

The front door opened yet again. As crazy as things got around here, Polly was having a blast.

Two very young men came toward the kitchen, chattering at each other.

"Oh," the first said. "Hello. Is Jerry here yet? And what's that container out there? Big load of lumber? Because wow, dude. That's some serious construction."

"Hi Doug," Henry said. "Jerry isn't here yet and that container is Polly's stuff from Boston. Do you want coffee?"

Polly remembered the kid's name - Doug Randall. His friend was Billy Endicott.

Doug shuddered. "None of that black sludge for me. Got my pop in the cooler here. Are you getting a fridge when the electricity's done?" he asked Polly.

"You bet," she said. "And then I'll even stock whatever soda you want."

"You live in Iowa now," Henry said. "It's pop."

"That's right," Polly said. "Pop. I'll practice."

"So you're moving in now?" Doug asked. "This place is still kind of rustic. You should rent an RV or something if you want to live in Bellingwood."

"No," Polly replied. "I'm not moving in yet. I'm just getting my things out of storage. I already had to buy new clothes. I kept running out before I had time to go to the laundromat."

"You bought new clothes to do construction?" Doug asked.

She bit her lips together. She wasn't prepared to admit to these men that she mostly bought underthings, but he was right. She'd gotten three new pairs of jeans and they were already quite comfortable from being worn and washed all the time. "I'm a girl, Doug. We buy clothes to do everything."

As ridiculous as that sounded to Polly, it appeased him.

"What are you boys doing standing around?" Jerry Allen asked, coming in to the kitchen.

Doug and Billy both jammed the rest of their cinnamon rolls in their mouths and Jimmy Rio tossed his empty coffee cup into the trash can. Sam Terhune re-filled his and the two headed for the stairway.

Jerry laughed as the area emptied. "Did I do that? I was just kidding. Looks like Polly's taking care of us again today."

She put her hand out and he shook it. "If you're working on

my house, the least I can do is feed you. I'm excited about finishing the kitchen."

"Excuse me, Miss Giller?"

Polly turned to the two young movers. "Are you ready for me?"

"Yeah. If you'll show us where you want your things, we'll unload the container. Thanks for the rolls and coffee."

She put her hand on Jerry's arm. "I'll be back after I get them started. Help yourself.

Henry walked with her as she followed the movers.

She blinked as she thought about what he'd said earlier. "Do you really think we should put the bed upstairs already?"

He shrugged. "Why not? We'll have the bathroom done up there next month. You won't be able to move into the apartment until we finish the kitchen and put the new flooring down, but that shouldn't stop you from living in the building. There are plenty of rooms for you to choose from."

"I'd have more privacy in the middle bedroom, wouldn't I?"

"That's what I was thinking. There are a lot of windows in those rooms. We can run power over to you so you can have a lamp and a clock."

"I thought I'd be in the Ames apartment for at least six months. It's nice, but living here would be easier. And maybe I could get to know more people in town, too."

"Man, I'm an idiot," Henry said.

"What?"

"I'm sorry. I should have asked if you wanted to have dinner with my family this weekend. At least you could have met somebody."

She laughed. "But they're not from around here any longer, are they?"

"Got me there," he said. "I'm sorry I didn't even think about that, though. You have to be pretty lonely all by yourself."

"Not really," Polly said, shaking her head. "I've always been kind of a loner. I like doing things by myself. Lately, I'm so tired I have just about enough time after dinner to fall into bed before

I'm asleep. I haven't watched television or read a book in weeks." She clenched her fist and flexed. "I'm starting to build up some muscle, though. It's good for me."

Henry bent down and pushed a big rock in place to hold the door open. "Right in here, guys. Follow me and I'll show you the space we cleared. Leave the mattress and box springs up here, though. I'll have you take those upstairs."

Polly watched him manage the movers. This Henry Sturtz fellow was a pretty good guy. She recognized that the day she first met him. He made it fun for her to be involved in renovating this old place. There was always something for her to do and he didn't treat her like a delicate flower. Steve had been over a couple of times, but that had been in the first two weeks. Once he realized that Polly had everything in hand, he dropped into the background again.

There were times she could hardly believe this was her life, but then she couldn't imagine doing anything else.

CHAPTER FOURTEEN

Mid-September

Muttering curses to herself, Polly shuddered at Sal's email message: *"Call when you see this. Joey's been asking about you."*

The last thing she wanted to deal with was more of Joey's insanity. The post office still forwarded her mail and at least twice a week there was a long missive from him, wondering where she'd gone and what she was doing. He'd begged and pleaded, cajoled and even hinted at threats as the weeks went on. She prayed no one would tell him where she'd gone. The good news was that he really didn't have a connection with any of her friends.

She'd made Bunny swear to never tell him a thing. That had been a ridiculous conversation. Bunny simply couldn't understand why Polly didn't want to be part of the Delancy family. The family was quite wealthy and well-respected in Boston society.

The truth was that the only one who carried any respect was Joey's father and he did his best to avoid being part of the family activities. Joey's mother was on many committees and knew people because of that, but Polly never knew her to spend time with friends. The woman was a little odd. It had been so strange when Joey was arrested. They'd sent a high-priced lawyer to deal with the situation, but otherwise ignored the entire event. It was almost as if they believed as long as they didn't acknowledge it, the situation hadn't actually happened. Joey had done the same thing, Polly realized, when he stopped going to the counseling sessions and anger-management course the court prescribed for him. The whole family had a blind spot - no one was willing to take responsibility for Joey's problem.

She knew better than to open the letters that came, but it was like watching a horrible train wreck over and over. At some level, Polly hoped he'd give up and understand they weren't ever going to be together. The letters were beginning to slow down and Polly hoped that one day, he'd finally give up. She came to Iowa to start a new life and he had no part in it. For the first time in a long time, Polly was involved in something much bigger than her own small life. She hadn't gotten to know people in town yet, but that would come. It was fun just becoming reacquainted with the area.

Polly leaned back in the recliner. Moving day would happen soon. Henry had installed cabinets in the kitchen on the main level and appliances were arriving this week. The bathroom in her upstairs apartment was nearly complete. As soon as those two rooms were done, she'd be ready to set up her bed and move in. She didn't need much more than that.

She looked at her phone, took a deep breath and dialed her friend.

"Polly. There you are," Sal said. "I was wondering when I'd hear from you."

"Hey there," Polly responded. "How are you? Dating anyone fun?"

Sal laughed out loud. "Oh, you know. Blind dates and dimwits, though the young man who took me to the concert on Saturday wasn't half bad. He *is* a little worried that his mother might not like me."

"Why's that?"

"Because I'm so tall. Polly, he's only five-foot-six. He's adorable and sweet and a nice guy, but even if I wear flats, I tower over him. He said his mother is only four-foot-eight. My god, I'm a giant."

"Don't you let anyone tell you that you're too tall. You look good in four-inch stilettos."

"I know," Sal said. "I'll let him take me out for dinner one more time. If he's still uncomfortable about our height difference and says one more thing about how his mother will be intimidated by me, I'll put an end to it. How about you? Meeting any cute corn-fed boys out there?"

"Who has time for that? I'm putting up walls and finishing cabinets. I'm working hard."

"Of course you are. I thought you had a nice young man who was your contractor. Henry, is it?"

"Henry Sturtz. And yes, he's a good guy. But the best part is that he lets me do as much of the work as I want to do."

"You like that? My bookish, nerdy friend who loves Star Wars movies and video games? You're really getting your hands dirty?"

"If I want this place to be mine, I want it really to be mine." Polly huffed a laugh. "Honestly, what I mostly do is sweep up and keep things organized for them. I can *almost* tell you the difference between a drywall nail and a finishing nail. Almost. Don't test me, though. But when someone needs a new package of nails, I know what they're asking for and can go get it."

"So you're their gopher. That seems wrong since you're paying for everything."

"That's not it," Polly said. "Everybody does their own thing. I just pitch in when I can. It's a lot of fun." She took a breath. "Okay. You scared me. What did Joey do?"

"Tell me you talked to Bunny about not telling him where you are."

"I did. I made her promise."

"And Drea wouldn't say anything, right?"

"No. Why?"

"Somehow he got my phone number. The first time he called me, I didn't know who it was so I answered."

Polly's mouth went dry. "What did he say?"

"He asked if I knew where you were. I was so taken off guard, I said that of course I knew where you were. Then I realized that I'd just sealed my own fate."

"Tell me the rest."

"I hung up on him as soon as the words were out of my mouth."

Polly laughed. "You did what?"

"Yeah. I just hung up the phone. He called me right back, though and said that the call must have dropped. Then he asked me where you'd gone. I told him I didn't know and hung up again."

"You didn't," Polly said. "He called back, though, right?"

"Yeah. Said he must be in a bad location because the calls kept dropping. And then he said that he must have heard me wrong because he was sure I said that I knew where you were."

"Tell me you didn't hang up again."

"No. I told him that even though I knew where you were, if you didn't want him to know, I certainly wasn't telling him. He cried on the damned phone, Polly. He cried."

"Crap."

"He begged and pleaded with me to tell him. Apparently, you two are star-crossed lovers destined to be together, no matter what obstacles are placed in your path."

"Yeah. I've heard that one before. I'm so sorry. I didn't want you to have to be involved in this mess."

"Better me than anyone else. I told him that he wasn't going to get any information out of me and then I hung up."

"He called back?"

"Not that day. He called the next day. That time I recognized the phone number and ignored it. But he called four times just to make sure I wasn't going to answer. He finally left a voice mail asking me to call. He just wanted to talk to someone who loved you as much as he did."

"Oh joy," Polly said. "I'm sorry."

"He called the next day about the same time - probably his lunch break. I answered and told him to stop harassing me - that I wasn't going to give him any information about you. If you had wanted him to know where you were, you would have told him. He didn't like that answer."

"He wouldn't. The guy is nuts."

"Yeah. He showed up at my work this morning."

Polly sat up straight. "He what? How does he even know where you work? I never told him anything about you."

"I'm not sure. But I told the security guard not to let him in again. And I made sure Joey knew that he wasn't welcome there. I also told him that if I ever saw him again, I was going to get the police involved and charge him with harassment. But Polly, he's looking for you. You might want to let Bunny and Drea know that they need to keep their wits about them. He's persistent. Really persistent. It's kind of creepy."

"I don't know how to make him stop," Polly said.

"Neither do I," Sal replied. "Maybe you write him a letter."

"I can't mail a letter from Iowa. He'd know where to find me."

"No. Write it and send it to me. I'll post it from here in town to him. Tell him to leave you alone. That you've left the state and are finished with him. That he's never supposed to contact you again. That you don't love him and never will. And maybe put a warning in there to leave your friends alone. What do you think about that?"

Polly slid back into the recliner and tucked her legs up underneath her. "What I think is that this is completely weird. Who does this?"

"Joey Delancy."

"Sal," Polly said, "I really thought that if I just got far enough away from him and didn't respond to any of his letters, he'd give up. We haven't talked to each other in at least six months."

"I wish this weren't happening to you, girlfriend. Can you think of anything else I can do to help? Do you want me to sic my short boyfriend on him?"

Polly laughed. "Only if he's a scary lawyer or maybe part of the mob."

"Nope. Neither of those things."

"You're probably right about me writing him a letter. I'll do that. Thanks for mailing it for me."

"No problem. Maybe I'll drive up to New Hampshire or Maine and post it from there. That would throw him off the scent." Sal giggled. "I know. I'll send it to my cousin in Florida. She'd post it for us."

Polly went quiet.

"What are you thinking about, missy?" Sal asked.

"I was thinking that if he went to Florida, maybe he'd get chomped up by an alligator. I wouldn't have to ever worry about him again."

"I don't think it's going to be that easy."

"Me either. I have a bad feeling that Joey is going to torment me for a long time. Man, when I pick 'em, I really do it up right."

"Don't get down on yourself," Sal said. "You've never run into anything like him before. Sure, you dated a couple losers, but haven't we all?" She laughed. "I know I've had my fair share. But you dated some nice guys in there, too. Besides, Joey didn't seem all that bad when you first met him. I thought he was pretty okay."

"It's hard to believe I was so blind."

Sal chuckled. "Not really. You believe the best about people."

"I suppose."

"The thing is, most of us want to be what you believe us to be. Before I met you, I thought I had two choices. I was either going to end up just like my mother - some snooty woman with too much money who looked down her nose at the rest of the world or ..." Sal paused.

"Or?"

"Or I was going to marry some bohemian type just to infuriate her. But then I moved in with you. It had never occurred to me that I could just be Sal Kahane and do whatever I wanted with my life. My mother didn't define me. Nobody did but me."

Polly felt tears threaten. "I didn't know that."

"Of course you didn't. You just treated me like you treat everyone and I wanted to be the person you thought I was. Independent and smart."

"And sexy and beautiful."

"Well those are just a given. Am I right?" Sal's laughter rang across the phone.

"You're absolutely right."

"I miss you, Polly," Sal said. "I know that you are exactly where you're supposed to be, but I wish you were still here. I want to make you meet these silly boys that my mother keeps expecting me to marry. Heck, maybe one of them would be perfect for you. So far, they're not doing me any good."

"Maybe you should tell your mother to stop setting you up."

"Like that will happen. And besides, with all these choices, surely the odds are going to be in my favor at some point."

"I just want to know how she manages to find so many. My goodness, who knew there were even that many single men in the entire state of Massachusetts?"

"Hey," Sal protested.

"Well, I'm not wrong. She has fresh fodder for you every weekend, it seems. Where does that woman come up with them?"

"She has no shame when it comes to asking her friends about their sons and grandsons. Good grief, Polly, I'm getting grandsons. And those poor boys. They have no idea what kind of woman they're meeting."

"If I were any one of them, I'd be terrified the minute I met you."

"That's the image I like. Sal Kahane - the woman who strikes terror in the very hearts of all young male Boston Jews."

Polly cackled. "At their Bar Mitzvahs, they're all warned about you. Rabbis everywhere tell tales of the single Sal Kahane."

"I dated a rabbi a couple of weeks ago. He was nice, but wow, total nerd. He wanted to talk about physics all night. Something about how physics was the basis for the beginning of creation. I just stared at him."

"Was he attractive?"

"That's why I was staring. It wasn't like I was getting into a deep discussion about God and physics. But he was kind of handsome."

"So why aren't you still dating him?"

"He wants to get married and have lots of children."

"I thought the purpose of these dates was to find you a husband."

"You might think that," Sal said. "Mother might think that. But I'm not quite as ready as she is. And besides, don't you think it's odd for him to ask my intentions regarding marriage and children on the first date?"

"Maybe a little. So no second date?"

"Nah. When I told him that I wasn't ready to be married quite yet, he thanked me for my time. I didn't hear from him again."

"I don't know how you do it," Polly said. "I'd be insane if I had to date that many men. For now, I'm just glad to be on my own."

"And you're doing that very well. I miss you terribly, but I'm proud of you. Are you going to send me a letter for Joey?"

"Yeah. I'll do it. Hopefully I can come up with just the right words to make him go away."

"You're good at words," Sal said. "You've got this. I should go. I need to finish an article tonight. Send me more pictures of what you're doing out there. So far, I'm still not seeing it."

"I will. I love you, Sal."

"I love you too, sweetie. Be good.".

CHAPTER FIFTEEN

Mid-October

Each morning when she woke and looked out of the immense windows in the old school, Polly knew she was finally home. The leaves on the massive sycamore trees along the creek were in the midst of their fall transformation and the yellows, oranges, reds and greens were beautiful. She checked the time. Six o'clock. No reason to hurry. Moving into the old school house shaved time from her morning ritual, but the last thing Polly wanted to do was get caught in the shower across the hall when workmen arrived.

The apartment was coming along. The built-in bookshelves of her soon-to-be living room were finished. Henry did beautiful work and for the first time, she thought that maybe all her books might be able to have their own homes. She'd left boxes of books with her father when she moved to Boston for good. Who needed a private library when you worked in a public library every day? Truth was, she missed her books.

Her stomach growled and she sat up and slipped her feet into the slippers beside the bed. She'd showered last night after spending the entire day painting the front room. Those high ceilings made for many trips up and down the ladder, but she was going to finish it today. Polly pulled her robe on, gathered up a pile of clothes she'd set out last night and walked across the cavernous hallway to the apartment and into the bathroom. Looking in the mirror, she giggled at herself.

"That's why you don't wash your hair before you go to bed, Giller. Doesn't matter what you do, it never works out well for you." She opened a drawer and took out her brush, yanked it through her hair until it was free of rats, and then dug around for a hair tie. She'd only been in this bathroom a short time and the drawers were already a disorganized mess. "You're useless. No one can ever see what you've done here. It's embarrassing."

Jamming the drawer shut, she opened another one and took out her toothpaste. While brushing her teeth, Polly thought back to the previous October. She hadn't met Joey yet - that happened in November. It had just been another normal day. Get up, go to work and maybe do something with a friend after work. What a difference a year made. For that matter, what a difference six months had made. Six months ago she moved back to Iowa and here she was, living in a place that was all hers. It was a chaotic mess of a place right now, but it was hers. Every day she woke up, something different happened. She'd learned more about construction and renovation than she ever thought she would know.

Polly changed into jeans and a t-shirt, shaking her head at the paint spatters on her clothes. Her father would be proud of the work she was doing. One thing she learned from him was how to work hard. When she dropped into bed at night, she was always exhausted. Whether it was hauling out trash or helping to move appliances or furniture, carrying things up and down stairs for the workmen or painting, Polly insisted on being part of it. Henry was always agreeable. It was like he understood her need to make this building hers. She knew better than to get in his way, and had asked more than once if he needed her to just back off. But he was willing to teach her how to do anything she wanted to do.

The one place he did encourage her to stay far away from was plumbing. He introduced her to the plumbing contractor once, but Polly had promptly forgotten his name, especially when the grouchy man sputtered about ancient waste systems. All Polly cared about was that the bathrooms worked and she could run water for coffee. He'd done much more than that, but at least she hadn't needed to be involved.

Polly ran back across the hall, flung her robe and slippers at the bed and sagged against the door sill when they missed by a mile. Rolling her eyes, she pulled the door shut and headed for the stairs. It's not like she wasn't going to wear them again tonight and no one went in that room now that she was sleeping there. Who would know or care? She certainly didn't.

The main level of the old school house was still in chaos. Drywall would soon be going up, so the electricians were working as fast as possible to finish pulling wires. There should be a full house of workers in here today. She wished there was a bakery in town.

Looking through her cupboards, Polly decided the best she was pulling off this morning was biscuits. She'd picked up several jars of jams and jellies at a farmer's market earlier in the summer, so she put those out on the counter and started coffee. She should have done that first.

The sound of the front door opening sent Polly out into the hallway to see who was coming in this early. It wasn't even seven o'clock yet.

"Good morning, Polly," Henry Sturtz said. He set the two bags he'd carried in on the counter. "I had an early breakfast meeting in Boone, so I picked donuts up. I wanted to catch you before you started baking anything. Am I on time?"

She grinned. "Perfect timing. I was just starting to think about it. What's on deck today?"

"Mostly drywall. We should finish the offices today. If there's time, I'd like to begin framing the outer walls of the room across the hall. You don't know what you're going to do with that yet, do you?"

"No. I'm sorry. There are so many decisions and I haven't given much thought to what I want that space to look like."

"No worries."

Polly opened the cupboard and brought out several paper plates while Henry opened the bags of donuts.

"We can wait to put them out," she said, "but I'm starving. What did you get?"

He looked through the bags, then pushed one in front of her. "I know you like chocolate frosting and nuts. There are a couple in this one."

They'd only had donuts one other time and that was a couple of months ago. How he remembered that, Polly couldn't imagine, but she smiled and reached in with a napkin. "Thank you."

"People ask me if you're nervous living in this big old building all by yourself," Henry said. "I know it's only been a couple of weeks, but how is it?"

"Quiet." Polly smiled. "Sure, there are creaks and groans, but it is so quiet. I'd forgotten how much I missed that. Living out on the farm, I could go all night without hearing a car drive by. I love the quiet."

He chuckled. "But you really feel safe here all by yourself?"

She huffed a laugh. "I'm in Bellingwood. Who's going to hurt me? I lock the doors and ..." Polly shook her head. "This is Bellingwood. I walked around downtown Boston and didn't worry about people assaulting me, I feel perfectly safe here."

"You never know," Henry said, lifting his eyebrows. "Maybe there are ghosts in this old building."

"I'd have met them by now, don't you think?" Polly shook her head. "I'm safer here than I've been in a long time."

Henry frowned at her, but she didn't want to talk about Joey with him. She didn't want to talk about Joey with anyone out here.

He'd finally quit sending mail to her after she wrote to him, using Sal as her postal clerk. Polly told him it was over and that she'd left Boston. She told him that she had no feelings left at all for him and that he needed to find someone else. That seemed to have done the trick. Sal said that she heard nothing more from him and none of Polly's other friends had any communication with him. Hopefully, the entire thing was behind her now.

"What are you thinking about?" Henry asked. "You went quiet."

"Nothing." Polly gave her head a quick shake. She smiled. "I'm excited to be moving forward. This place looks like it might actually be finished one of these days. I have so many dreams and plans for it, but it's hard to focus when I'm overwhelmed by the details." She gestured down at her clothes. "And paint. There is a lot of painting left to be done."

"You're actually doing a nice job on that," Henry said. "As well as anyone I could have hired. You learned quickly."

"Dad hated painting, but we repainted all of the rooms in the house over the years. He was a stickler for perfection. 'Bout drove me nuts, but I guess I learned to do it right."

"I would have liked to have met him."

"He would have liked you," Polly said. She stepped out of the kitchen and walked with him through the main hallway across tarps laid out to protect the floors and around buckets and tools. "Dad would have loved being part of this. Sometimes I really miss him and wish he were here to help me make decisions." Polly stopped and put her hand on Henry's forearm. "You know. I appreciate the fact that you are so sensible. As much as I miss Dad, you've made the decisions pretty easy for me. When I started, I thought it was going to be much, much worse. What did I know about renovation on this scale?" She sighed. "What did I know about renovation at all? But you've never made me feel dumb. I appreciate that."

Henry shrugged. "No big deal. Just the way my dad taught me to do business. You and I are going to be living in the same town and we'll probably do more business through the years. If I mess this up now, it's the last time you'll want to work with me."

"I just wanted you to know that I'm glad we're working together," Polly said. "You've made this a lot of fun."

The front door opened and several men walked in.

"Hey boss," one of them said. "Coffee on?"

Henry gestured with his head toward the kitchen. "Should be almost done. There's donuts there, too." He smiled at Polly. "Looks like we'd best get to work."

"I need a big cup of coffee before I tackle those walls upstairs."

"You sure you don't want some help?"

Polly shook her head. "I've got it. I just need coffee."

~~~

After lunch Polly was back at it. She didn't often spend the lunch hour with the guys who were working on the building. She had a couple of times in the beginning, but as nice as they were, she could tell it made them uncomfortable. Whether it was because she was a woman or the owner, who knew. She'd made a quick sandwich and gone up to her bedroom.

The thing was, it probably sounded pathetic and lonely, but it wasn't at all. There was so much going on during the day - questions coming at her and decisions to make - that having one hour when she didn't need to think about anything was a nice break. Once this building got a little closer to being finished, Polly knew she needed to find a way to meet people in town. The time would come.

Her phone buzzed in her back pocket and Polly put the paint brush on the ladder step above her before taking the phone out.

"Hey there," she said to Sal, while stepping gingerly down the ladder.

"I was just thinking about you, wondering if you were lonely yet."

"Not yet," Polly said. "But that's funny. I was just thinking about how I needed to figure out how to meet people."

"Other than those ruffians renovating your little schoolhouse?"

"Don't be that way," Polly admonished her friend. "They're not ruffians and it isn't a little schoolhouse."

"Sorry. But you haven't met any new girlfriends?"

"Nobody that will ever take your place."

Sal laughed out loud. "Oh sweetie, there's not a soul in the world who could take my place. I'm one of a kind. You know that. You don't need me to come out and rescue you?"

"I'm really quite happy," Polly said. "And I don't know if Iowa is ready for you."

"Maybe we could meet in the middle. You should fly to Philadelphia and I'd come down."

"That's not the middle."

"It's about as far west as I dare come," Sal said. "If I cross the Mississippi, the entire Eastern seaboard might break off into the Atlantic."

Polly chuckled. "You really are just calling to see if I'm lonely? Nothing else?"

"Maybe I was lonely for you. But otherwise, that's it. How's the place coming?"

"Pretty good. I'm painting the rooms upstairs." Polly had kept Sal apprised of the changes, sending pictures and details of the renovation. It was strange to realize that she didn't have that many friends who cared about what she was doing here. But that would change.

"Do you have paint in your hair?"

Polly reached up and patted her head. Sure enough, she brought her hand away with blotches of paint on it. "Either I just put it there or I'm a messy painter."

"I'll let you get back to work. I just wanted to say hello."

"Hello to you and thanks for calling. I'll talk to you later?"

"Call when you can. Love you, girlfriend."

"Love you, too."

Polly put the phone back in her pocket. She did miss Sal.

~~~

"Hey Polly."

She looked down at Henry who had walked into the room. "Yeah?"

"We're out of here for the day. Everyone else is gone."

"It's that time? Wow."

He shook his head. "No. I'm letting them go a little early. Everybody has a lot going on tonight for some reason or other." Henry looked down at his phone. "I just got a call from my neighbor. Her back door is stuck and she can't get it open."

She chuckled. "You get to fix it for her?"

"It's what we Sturtz men do. Dad took care of her for years and now that he's in Arizona, it's my job. I told her I'd be there soon. Are you okay alone?"

Polly scowled at him. "Yes."

"I was just checking. Do you want me to lock up?"

She shook her head. "No. I think UPS has some deliveries coming. Just leave it. I'll lock up later."

"You're sure?"

This time, Polly turned the scowl into a glare. "I'm perfectly capable …"

Henry interrupted her, laughing. "I know. I know. I was kidding. See you in the morning?"

"Yeah. I'll see you. Have a good evening."

With everyone gone, the building grew quiet again - no more saws, nail guns or sanders making noise. Polly let her mind wander in the silence, wondering at the possibilities for this building and about the people she might meet. Maybe she'd get a dog. That was always a good way to meet people. They were friendly enough around here that they'd smile and say hello if she took the dog for a walk.

She continued to paint, moving the ladder along the wall. It just wouldn't take that much effort on Polly's part. Even though she couldn't remember a single name of anyone she'd met except for Henry and a few of the other guys who worked for him, people in Bellingwood were friendly. Now that she lived in town, maybe she'd eat at the diner more often. The steak place out on the highway looked good and somebody mentioned that the general store sold homemade ice cream.

Polly laughed at herself. The library. She hadn't been in there yet. It wasn't open all the time, but maybe they'd let her volunteer. So many possibilities ahead. She just needed to get out and meet people.

She lifted her hand to take another swipe with the paintbrush, when all of a sudden …

"Hallooo! Is anyone here?"

Polly nearly fell off the ladder hearing a voice come from the main level, then muttered, "I'm going to have to get a dog."

~~~

This novella is a prequel to the Bellingwood series which starts with *All Roads Lead Home*. The best way to continue is to look for the Bellingwood Boxed Set #1, which contains the first three books in the series and a short Bellingwood Christmas story.

Polly Giller's life in Bellingwood is filled with fun, friendship and mysteries. In *All Roads Lead Home*, a mystery that has long haunted the community is uncovered and Joey Delancy arrives in town, threatening to disrupt everything Polly has built. You won't want to miss a single minute of her life. Start reading today.

THANK YOU FOR READING!

I'm so glad you enjoy these stories about Polly Giller and her friends. There are many ways to stay in touch with Diane and the Bellingwood community.

You can find more details about Sycamore House and Bellingwood at the website: http://nammynools.com/

Join the Bellingwood Facebook page:
https://www.facebook.com/pollygiller
for news about upcoming books, conversations while I'm writing and you're reading, and a continued look at life in a small town.

Be sure to sign up for the newsletter to receive information about upcoming books, events, and other exciting Bellingwood news. Included in every newsletter is a short story that offers a glimpse into the lives of Bellingwood residents who interact daily with Polly Giller.

Diane Greenwood Muir's Amazon Author Page is a great place to watch for new releases.

Follow Diane on Twitter at twitter.com/nammynools for regular updates and notifications.

Recipes and decorating ideas found in the books can often be found on Pinterest at: http://pinterest.com/nammynools/

And, if you are looking for Sycamore House swag, check out Polly's CafePress store: http://www.cafepress.com/sycamorehouse

Made in the USA
Lexington, KY
25 June 2017